CHAPTER ONE

THE WORST FINALLY happened on an otherwise unremarkable Tuesday afternoon in the middle of a gray and sullen British spring.

It wasn't as if Lexi Haring hadn't been expecting it. They'd all been on tenterhooks since the news had come in. After all these years—and all the appeals that the Worth family solicitors had assured everyone were nothing but noise right up until the very end— Atlas Chariton was a free man.

Not just free. *Innocent.*

Lexi had watched the press conference he'd given, right there in front of the American prison where he'd been serving a life sentence with no possibility of parole for the murder that DNA evidence at his last appeal trial had conclusively proved he didn't commit. He'd been released the same day.

She hadn't been able to turn away from a single moment of the breathless coverage, if she was honest, and not only because every channel was showing the press conference live.

"I've maintained my innocence from the start," Atlas had said in that dark, powerful voice of his that had seemed to come straight through the screen, the English he spoke with both a British accent and that hint of his native Greek as richly mysterious to her ears as ever. He'd had the same effect on her he always had. He filled the small bedsit Lexi counted herself lucky to have in her shabby West London neighborhood. It was a long bus ride plus ten minutes' brisk walk to the Worth estate where she worked, thanks to her uncle's continuing kindness to her. And even if she sometimes felt her uncle wasn't all that kind, she kept it to herself and tried to remind herself of that luck. "I am delighted to be proved so beyond any possible remaining doubt."

Atlas looked older, which was only to be expected, though no gray had dared yet invade that thick black hair of his that threatened to curl at any moment. The stark ferocity that had always been there on his face and stamped into the long, lean lines of his body was more evident now, eleven years after he'd first been arrested. It made his black eyes gleam. It made his cruel mouth seem even harsher and more brutal.

He made Lexi shiver the way he always had done, though he was all the way on the other side of the Atlantic Ocean. Her heart kicked at her the way it always had when he was near. And it was as if he was aiming that pitiless midnight stare directly at her, straight through the television cameras.

She thought he was. Of course he was.

She had no doubt that he knew perfectly well that she was watching.

It reminded her of the way he'd glared at her a decade ago, when she'd been eighteen and overwhelmed and had stuttered every time her gaze had clashed with his across that overheated, airless courtroom on Martha's Vineyard. And yet she'd still somehow managed to choke out the testimony that had damned him.

She could still remember every word she'd said. She could taste each one on her tongue, bitter and thick.

She remembered too much of that time. The intense pressure her uncle and cousins had put on her to testify when she hadn't wanted to—when she'd been desperate to believe there was another explanation. That there had to be another explanation.

And the way Atlas had watched her in that stony, furious silence when she'd broken down on the stand and admitted she couldn't think of one.

"What will you do now?" a reporter had asked him outside the prison.

Atlas's mouth had curved, lethal and cold, more dangerous than the sharpest knife. Lexi had felt it deep in her belly as if he'd thrust it into her, steel edge to hard hilt. No one could possibly mistake it for a smile, surely. No one could miss the fact it was a weapon.

It was her curse that even now, even after everything that had happened, he was the only man alive who made her heart skip a beat, then pound, long and low.

"I will live my life," Atlas had said, dark and sure, a terrible promise. "At last."

Lexi had known what that meant. What was coming as surely as night followed day. Her uncle Richard had hemmed and hawed and blustered rather than face the subject head-on, but she thought he'd known, too. Her cousins Gerard and Harry, meanwhile, had acted as if it wasn't happening. The same way they'd acted eleven years ago when Philippa had been found dead in the pool at Oyster House, the family's summer estate in Martha's Vineyard. The way they'd behaved through the trial and the appeals process all this time, as if they weren't involved. As if it would all go away and revert to normal if they pretended nothing had happened in the first place.

And as if there had ever been any possibility that a

man like Atlas would simply fade away into the ether, in jail or out.

Lexi had always known better. When she'd wanted desperately to believe in his innocence and when she'd reluctantly believed in his guilt. Because to her, no matter what, Atlas Chariton had always been the only man in all the world.

"The last thing he's going to want to do is take up where he left off," irascible Harry told anyone who would listen in the Worth family home and offices peppered throughout the grand old stately house and estate that had been in the family for hundreds of years, spread across the acreage that had been gloriously maintained in West London since the seventeenth century. Harry was always that confident, about everything. "I'm sure he's got as little interest in us as we do in him."

But Lexi knew better. She'd been the one up in that witness box. She'd been the one who'd watched Atlas's face as she'd testified against him. So harsh and terrible. All judgment and the promise of retribution.

At the time she'd convinced herself it was a measure of the man himself. The signs he was a killer, right there in his grim gaze and that set to his proud jaw—and that despite the more tender, secret things she'd felt about him then.

A schoolgirl's crush, she'd told herself then, to excuse herself. That was all.

Today it felt like an indictment. That she'd had a desperate, endless crush on a man like Atlas and had testified against him the way she had—had she really been telling the truth to the best of her ability? Had she bowed to her uncle's whim the way she always did? Or had she simply wanted to get Atlas's attention however she could, linking herself to him forevermore?

She didn't know how to answer that.

Or to be more truthful, she didn't want to know the answer to that.

Whatever her emotions, the science told the truth. There was no getting around it, much as she might have wanted to, in some desperate attempt to feel better about what she'd done. She'd thought she'd been standing up for Philippa, doing the right thing even if it had torn her up inside, and she'd hated herself for the part of her that had ached for the Atlas she'd thought she'd known, but now...

Now she would pay. Of that she had no doubt.

She'd had the weeks between his release and his arrival in London to reconsider every thought she'd ever had about Atlas, and to cast herself in the light he most assuredly saw her, which was in no way flattering to either the teenager she'd been or the woman she was these days.

And now he was here.

Lexi forced a smile and nodded at the wide-eyed secretary who'd brought her the news.

"Thank you for coming all the way out here to tell me," she said, and was proud of how calm she sounded. How serene and capable, as if this disaster was happening to someone else.

"Mr. Worth wanted me to tell you especially," the secretary told her, her northern vowels sounding extra pronounced, as if the heightened tension around the estate over these past weeks was getting to her and bringing out her Yorkshire.

Lexi could sympathize. She kept her smile steady as she looked past the other woman, out toward the great, green sweep of the lower lawn and the straight march of the famous drive that led to the grand sprawl of Worth Manor in all its ancient splendor. It had once been the pride of a very rich merchant and the impoverished noblewoman he'd married and tried to win with the things his money could do, and sometimes Lexi liked to imagine that the estate itself was ripe with all that old longing time had not assuaged. Today was another gray, wet day in a long run of the same, with only the desperately cheerful flowers along the borders of the winding drive to suggest that spring was limping along.

There were two vehicles parked outside. One was the little sedan that the secretary had driven down from the manor house, small and nondescript. The other was a gleaming black, classic Jaguar convertible that looked like it deserved its own Bond film. If not a franchise.

Her stomach lurched, then knotted, and she felt pale all the way through. But it wouldn't do to show any of that.

Nor would it help.

"If you hurry back," Lexi said in the same deliberately, preternaturally calm voice, because she had nothing else to work with today except the appearance of serenity, "you might beat the rain."

The secretary nodded her thanks, pulling her serviceable mackintosh tighter around her sturdy torso and letting herself out of Lexi's small office. Lexi stayed where she was. Frozen solid, in fact. Lexi could hear the secretary's heels click loudly against the uneven floorboards as she moved down the hall toward the front door.

Lexi's office, such as it was, was far away from the main part of the estate and the manor house itself. She spent her days out in what had once been a carriage house, separated from the family and the estate's hundreds of daily visitors as much as it was possible to be while still on the same property. Her cousins lived on the estate, of course—Gerard and his family ensconced in the residential wing of Worth Manor as befit the heir to everything, and Harry in one of the cottages where he could come and go and drink as he pleased. Neither one of them had ever shown the slightest interest in leaving home or exploring the world outside of a few years at university.

Philippa had been the only member of the family who'd wanted something—anything—different. She'd been nineteen when she'd died, filled with plans and dreams and a wild, unmanageable and overwhelming certainty about how beautiful her life was going to be if she could just start living it. She'd found her father tyrannical and the expectations placed on her as the only Worth daughter enervating.

More than that, she'd been kind and silly and fiercely loyal, and Lexi missed her. Every day.

Lexi reminded herself of Philippa when she was tempted to harbor dark thoughts about her uncle and cousins—something she tried to talk herself out of almost as soon as they occurred, because she thought it made her a very small person indeed if she allowed herself to be as ungrateful as she felt sometimes. Too often, in fact. Uncle Richard had been unduly kind to her when she was nothing to him but a niece he hardly knew, who he could easily have written off the way he had her mother.

Richard had never approved of his challenging and problematic sister Yvonne's marriage to unreliable partier Scott Haring. Much less the desperate, squalid life his sister went on to lead with a man so weak and fatally flawed. And yet there he'd been the day Lexi's parents had finally succumbed to their addictions, ready to scoop her up and give her a life.

Of course she was grateful for that. She would always be grateful for that.

And on the days it was hard to feel grateful while she did the work her cousins and uncle blew off, again, and then repaired to her grotty little flat while they lounged about in luxury, it was helpful to remind herself that

Philippa would have viewed everything about Lexi's life as a grand adventure. Literally everything. The bedsit in a neighborhood where Lexi could come and go anonymously and as she pleased. The commute to work on buses and along streets filled with regular Londoners going about their regular lives. These were things Philippa, raised in a very specific sort of high society bubble, catered to and sheltered in turn, would have found nothing short of magical.

Even this, Lexi thought as she heard the carriage house door open and shut again with rather more force than usual, and then the secretary's startled gasp as punctuation.

She knew exactly who'd arrived to face her at last, with no American courts or attorneys or bailiffs to keep her safe from him. Not even the marginal, grudging support of her uncle and cousins. Not this time.

It was finally happening, after the gnawing worry of the past decade and the wild panic of the past few weeks.

Her worst nightmare was coming true at last.

Atlas was here.

She heard the heavy, obviously male tread of his feet in the hall outside her door. Was it her imagination, or did he sound as if he was made of stone? As if he'd really and truly turned into the monster they'd made him—*she'd* made him—after all his years away?

And now that it was finally happening, she didn't know what to do with herself. Should she stand? Remain seated? Hide in her cramped little coat closet and wait for him to go away—delaying the inevitable?

She knew what she wanted to do, and glanced at her closet as if she might dive for it. But Lexi had never had the option to hide herself away from the unpleasant things in life. That was what happened when a girl was left to raise herself while her parents chased dragons wherever they led, which was never anywhere good. And it was what happened when she was then brought to live with a new family who treated her well enough, in the sense that they provided for her, but never, ever let her imagine that she was one of them.

But that veered toward ungrateful, she told herself as steadily as she could when the world was ending. And she wasn't ungrateful. She couldn't be.

Because then she'd be no better than her lost mother. And she'd spent her whole life trying her best to be nothing at all like Yvonne Worth Haring, once a sparkling heiress with the world at her feet, who'd died in squalor like any other junkie.

Lexi refused to start down that path, and she knew— she remembered too vividly—that the road to her mother's hell was liberally paved with ingratitude and all of it aimed straight at her uncle.

The heavy tread stopped outside her door and her heart pounded at her, so hard it made her feel dizzy. Lexi was suddenly glad she'd stayed in her seat, tucked up behind the narrow desk she used because a full-size desk wouldn't have fit in the small room. She wasn't sure her legs would have held her upright.

And she was having enough trouble keeping her heart from clawing its way out from behind her ribs without adding a collapse to the situation.

The door swung open, slow and ominous, and then he was there.

Right there.

Right here, she thought wildly, panic and dread exploding into something else, something sharper and all too familiar, as she sat there, struck dumb, unable to do anything but stare back at him.

Atlas.

Here.

He filled up the door to her tiny office with rather more brawn and heft than she remembered. He'd always been sculpted and athletic, of course. It was one of the reasons he'd been so beloved all over Europe in his heyday, and hadn't exactly helped her with the red-faced longing she'd tried so hard to hide. Another reason Europe had adored him was his epic rise from nothing and the power he'd gathered along the way—but Lexi thought his inarguable male beauty had helped that fascination along.

It had been difficult for her to get past way back when. It still was.

She recalled every inch of him, even if memory had muted him a little. In person he was bright, hot, unmistakable. That bold nose that made his profile so intense. The belligerent jaw and curiously high cheekbones that should have canceled each other out but instead came together to make him a little too extraordinary for her poor, overtaxed heart.

He'd had all that ten years ago. He had it all still, though it was all…different, somehow. He was still beautiful, certainly, male and hard and clearly as lethal as he was mouthwateringly handsome. But it was a harder and more intense sort of beauty today. A storm rather than a work of art.

As altered as he was.

Lexi felt as if his hands were wrapped tight around her neck, holding her breath for her. *This close* to doing exactly what she'd accused him of doing ten years ago.

Any second now, she'd start to choke…but not yet. She was frozen solid. Panicked from her head to her feet and unable to do a single thing but stare at him, the apparition from her own personal hell.

Atlas stood in the door to her office and filled it up, all flashing black eyes and that pugilistic set to his brutal jaw. He wore a dark, obviously bespoke suit that clung to his shoulders and made her far too aware of their size and sculpted, muscled width. As if he could not only bear the weight of the world on them if he chose, he could block it out, as well. He was doing that now.

He had always had that rough, impossible magnetism. It had rolled from him wherever he went, making the hair on the back of Lexi's neck stand up straight whenever he'd been near. Making it hard to breathe when he entered a room. Making her so aware of him that it was like a body ache.

The ache had kept her awake some nights, tucked away beneath the eaves in the manor house, where she'd lived in the servant's quarters and had been expected to find her circumstances evidence of her uncle's generosity. It hadn't exactly faded in the years since—it had just shifted into the nightmares that woke her in her tiny little bedsit and some nights, kept her from falling back to sleep.

He was far more compelling now. Brutally, lethally compelling. There was something untamed and dangerous about him that his luxurious suit did nothing to hide. If anything, the expertly tailored coat and trousers called attention to how wild he was, how much *more* he was than other men. He was so much bigger. Rougher. Infinitely more dangerous though he wore the disguise of civility with such ease.

And he glared at her as if he, too, was imagining what it would be like to take her apart with his own two hands.

She couldn't blame him.

Lexi's throat was so dry it hurt.

Her palms felt damp and her face was too hot. She had the vague notion she might be sick, but there was something in the pitiless way he regarded her that kept her from succumbing to the creeping nausea.

"Lexi," he murmured, her name an assault. An indictment. And he knew it. She could see he knew it, that it was a deliberate blow. That he reveled in it—but then, he'd earned that, too. "At last."

"Atlas."

She was proud of the way she said his name. No catch in her voice. No shakiness. No stutter. As if she was perfectly composed.

All a lie, of course, but she'd take anything at this point. Anything that got her through this. If there was any *getting through* something like this.

He didn't say anything else. He didn't step farther into her office. He only stood where he was and regarded her in that same nearly violent way, all terrible promise and impending threat.

It was excruciating.

"When did you arrive in London?" she asked, still managing to keep her voice calm. If thin.

One dark brow rose, and she felt it like a slap.

"Small talk?" His voice was harshly incredulous and made her feel small. Or small*er*. "I arrived this morning, as I'm certain you know full well."

Of course she knew. He'd been all over the news the moment his plane had set down in Heathrow.

Lexi wasn't the only one who couldn't seem to get enough of the scandalous rise and fall of Atlas Chariton. A man who'd built himself from nothing, then swept into the world of high-society high stakes as if he'd been made for it. He'd been hired as the CEO of the Worth Trust at a shockingly young age and had overseen the major renovations and reorganization that had taken the grand old estate from its old, moldering status to a major recreation center for public use and in so doing, had made himself and everyone else very, very wealthy. He'd opened the famous, Michelin-starred restaurant on the grounds. He'd created the five-star hotel that had opened and run beautifully while he'd been incarcerated, thanks entirely to his vision and planning, a point the papers had made repeatedly. He'd started the new programs that had continued in his absence, going above and beyond the usual stately house home and garden tours, making Worth Manor and its grounds a premier London tourist and local destination.

And then he'd been convicted of murdering Philippa and put away.

They'd all been living off his vision ever since.

But by the look of him, Atlas had been living off something else entirely.

A black, dark fury, if Lexi had to guess.

"And how do you find the estate?" she asked, as if she hadn't taken his warning to heart.

Atlas stared at her until a new heat made her cheeks feel singed, and she felt very nearly lacerated by her own shame.

"I find that the fact you are all still standing, unchanged and wholly unruined, offends me," he growled. "Deeply."

"Atlas, I want to tell you that I—"

"Oh, no. I think not." His teeth bared in something she was not foolish enough to call a smile. She remembered what his smiles had looked like before. How they'd felt when he'd aimed them her way. They had never been like this. Ruthless and terrible in turn. "No apologies, Lexi. It's much too late for that."

She found herself rising then, as if she couldn't help herself. Maybe she simply couldn't *sit there* another moment, like some kind of small animal of prey. She smoothed down the front of her pencil skirt and hoped she looked the way she'd imagined she had this morning in her mirror. Capable. Competent. Unworthy of this kind of malevolent focus.

"I know you must be very angry," she began.

And he laughed. It was a hard, male sound that rolled down the length of her spine and seemed to lodge itself there in her lower back, where it spread. Until there was that same old aching thing again, low in her belly and made of a kind of fire Lexi didn't pretend to understand.

But there was no getting around the fact that she'd never heard a laugh like that before. So utterly devoid of humor. So impossibly lethal she wanted to look down and check herself for bullet holes.

"You have no idea how angry I am, little girl," Atlas told her, that grim fury and something else making his black eyes gleam as they tore straight through her. "But you will. Believe me, you will."

CHAPTER TWO

ATLAS WAS USED to fury.

He was used to rage. That black, choking spiral that had threatened to drag him under again and again over the past decade and some years, very nearly had for good.

But this was different. She was different.

Because little Lexi Haring, who had once followed him around these very grounds like a shy puppy, all big eyes and a shy smile that was all for him, was the architect of his destruction.

Oh, he knew in some distant, rational part of his brain that she was no less a pawn than he had been in this. He knew exactly how little her relatives thought of her and more, what they'd taken from her. Her presence in this hidden away little carriage house made her status amongst the Worths perfectly clear, far away from the members of the family who mattered. More than that, he'd had his own investigators digging into these people for years now, gathering all the things he'd need when he was finally free, and he knew things about her he doubted she knew herself.

Things he'd always known he'd use against her without a second thought once the opportunity arose.

From the moment of his arrest Atlas had refused to accept that he'd never be free again. Some long, lonely years, that was all that had kept him sane in that loud, bright hell of concrete and steel.

And now, standing here in this drafty old place, he realized he remembered all the ins and outs of the Worth family dramas better than he'd like. All those memories of the way they'd excluded Lexi while pretending to extend her a little charity. Keeping her close enough to be grateful and uncertain, but never close enough to forget herself and the subservient place they wanted—needed—her to occupy.

But Atlas would be damned if he felt any sympathy for her. Lexi was the one who had sat up in that witness box and ruined him. One halting, obviously terrified word after the next.

He remembered her testimony too well. That and the way she'd looked at him, her wide brown eyes slicked with tears, as if it hurt her to accuse him of such things. And worse than that. With fear.

Of him.

The worst wasn't what she'd done to him. It was that unlike her bastard of an uncle, she'd believed that he'd done what he was accused of doing. She'd believed with all her heart and soul that he was a vicious killer. That he'd had an argument with impetuous, grandiose Philippa who had made no secret of the fact she'd have liked to get naked with him, had choked her because—the prosecution had thundered—he was a man with no impulse control and had feared that a relationship with the Worth heiress would get him fired, and had then thrown her into the pool on that cool summer night in the Oyster House compound.

Leaving her there to be found by Lexi when she'd gone looking for Philippa early the next morning.

"If Mr. Chariton feared that he would lose his position at the company because of Miss Worth, why would he leave her in the pool to be found the moment someone woke up?" his lawyer had asked Lexi.

Atlas could still remember the way her eyes had filled with tears. The way her lips had trembled. The way she'd looked at him, there at the defense table, as if he stormed through her nightmares nightly. As if he hadn't just killed Philippa, to her mind, but had broken her own heart, too.

"I don't know," she'd whispered. "I just don't know."

And in so doing, had made him the monster the jury had convicted after a mere two-hour deliberation.

It was Lexi's belief in the fact he must have done such a terrible thing—and how upset she'd been at the prospect—that had locked him away for a decade.

She might as well have turned the key in the lock herself.

"You've grown up," he said when it didn't look as if she planned to speak. Possibly ever again.

"I was eighteen when you left," she replied after a moment, her cheeks a crisp, hot red. "Of course I've grown up since then."

"When I *left*," he echoed her, his own words tinged with malice. "Is that what you call it? How delightfully euphemistic."

"I don't know what to call it, Atlas. If I could take back—"

"But you can't."

That sat there then, taking up all the space in the close little room, as claustrophobic and faintly shabby as it was possible to get on this vast, luxurious estate. And he understood exactly why her devious, manipulative uncle had stashed her away here. Heaven forfend she spend even one moment imagining herself on the same level as his feckless, irresponsible sons.

Atlas roamed farther inside the small office, cluttered

with overstuffed bookshelves and unframed prints when there were old masters piled high and unused in the attics of the great house. He was aware that it would take no more than an extra step to put himself right there on the opposite side of her flimsy little desk, within arm's reach. What bothered him was how very much he wanted to get close to her. Not just to make her uncomfortable, though he wanted that. Badly.

But he also wanted his hands on her. All over her, and not only because the past ten years had been so particularly kind to her—so kind, in fact, that he'd had to take a moment in the doorway to handle his reaction. And to remind himself that while he'd expected a drab little girl and had been wholly committed to doing what needed to be done with her, the fact she'd grown into something rather far removed from *drab* could only be to his benefit.

Because he had a very specific plan, she was integral to it, and it would involve more than just his hands. It would involve his entire body, and hers, and better still—her complete and total surrender to his will in all things.

He thought that might—just might—take the edge off.

Or anyway, it would be a good start.

And the fact she'd grown up curvy and mouthwatering just made it that much better.

"I don't know what to say." Lexi's voice was quieter then, and he watched, fascinated, as she laced her fingers together and held them in front of her as if they provided her with some kind of armor.

"Is this what wringing your hands actually looks like? I've never seen it in person before." He tilted his head slightly to one side as he let his gaze move over her bookshelves. All dull books about the damned house and the Worth family, stretching back centuries. It wasn't until he looked at her again that he saw the brighter and more cracked spines of the books behind her desk—within her reach—that suggested she allowed herself a little more fun than she perhaps wished to advertise. That boded well. "Is that meant to render me sympathetic?"

"Of course not. I only—"

"Here's the thing, Lexi." He stopped near the window and noted that the rain had begun again, because of course it had. This was England. He picked up one of the small, polished stones that lay on the sill, tested the weight of it in his hand, then set it down again. "You did not simply betray me, though let us be clear. You did. You also betrayed yourself. And worst of all, I think, Philippa."

She jerked at that, as if he'd hauled off and hit her. He wasn't that far gone. Not yet. He'd stopped imagining surrendering to the clawing need for brutality inside him some years into his prison term. Or he'd stopped imagining it quite so vividly as he had at first, anyway.

"Don't you think I know that?" she demanded, though it came out more like a whisper, choked and fierce at once. "I've done nothing since your release but go over it all in my head again and again, trying to understand how I could possibly have got it all so wrong, but—"

"Lucky for you, Philippa is just as dead now as she was eleven years ago," Atlas told her without the faintest shred of pity for her when she blanched at that. "She is the only one among us who does not have to bear witness to any of this. The miscarriage of justice. The incarceration of an innocent man. All the many ways this family sold itself out, betraying itself and me in the process. And in so doing, left Philippa's murder unsolved for a decade. Though there is one question I've been meaning to ask you for years now." He waited until she looked at him, her brown gaze flooded bright with emotion. *Good*, he thought. He hoped it hurt.

He waited another beat, purely for the theater of it. "Are you proud of yourself?"

Her throat worked for a moment, and he thought she might give in and let the tears he could see in her eyes fall—but she didn't. And he couldn't have said why he felt something like pride in that. As if it should matter to him that she had more control of herself these days than she had ten years back.

"I don't think anyone is proud of anything," she said, her voice husky with all those things he could see on her face.

"We are not speaking of *anyone*," Atlas said sternly. "Your uncle and your cousins will face a different reckoning, I assure you, and none of them deserve you rushing to defend them. I'm talking about you, Lexi. I'm talking about what *you* did."

He expected her to crumple, because the old version of Lexi had always seemed so insubstantial to him. In his memory she had been a shadow dancing on the edge of things. Always in the background. Always somewhere behind Philippa. She'd been eighteen and on the cusp of the beauty she hadn't grown into yet.

Though there had been no doubt she would. He'd known that even then, when he had made certain not to pay too close attention to the two silly girls who ran around the Worth properties together, always giggling and staring and making nuisances of themselves.

Her mouth had never seemed to fit her face, back then. Too lush, too wide. She'd been several inches shorter, if he wasn't mistaken, and she'd bristled with a kind of nervous, coltish energy that he knew had been her own great despair back then. Because she'd been so awkward next to her cousin, the languid and effortlessly blond Philippa.

They'd just been girls. He'd known that then, but it had

gotten confused across all these lost, stolen years. And still, Philippa had seemed so much older. Even though it was the always nervous Lexi who had actually done some real living in her early years, when she'd still been in the clutches of her addict parents.

Atlas hated that there was a part of him that still remembered the affection he'd once felt for the poor Worth relation. The little church mouse who the family had treated like their very own Cinderella, as if she ought to have been happy to dine off their scraps and condescension the rest of her life.

Looking at her now, it was clear that she was doing exactly that. That she'd taken it all to heart, locked away in the farthest reaches of the estate, where she could do all the work and remain out of sight and out of mind.

The way her uncle had always wanted it; and Atlas should have had more sympathy for her because of it.

He didn't.

She'd grown into her beauty now, however, though she appeared to be dressed like a mouse today. Or if he was more precise, a run-of-the-mill secretary in a sensible skirt and an unobjectionable blouse. Brown hair tugged into a severe bun that looked as if it ought to have given her a headache.

She looked as if she was dressed to disappear. To fade into the wallpaper behind her. To never, ever appear to have a single thought above her station.

But still, mouse or secretary or Cinderella herself, she didn't crumple, which made her far more brave than most of the men he'd met in prison.

"You will never know how sorry I am that my testimony put you behind bars," she said, her eyes slick with misery as if she was as haunted by all of this as he was. Yet she kept her gaze steady on his just the same. "But Atlas.

I didn't tell a single lie. I didn't make anything up. All I said was what I saw."

"What you saw." He let out a bitter laugh. "You mean what you twisted around in your fevered little teenage brain to make into some kind of—"

"It was what I saw, nothing more and nothing less." She pressed her lips together and shook her head. Once, harshly. Then again. "What did you expect me to do? Lie?"

"Certainly not." He moved until he was directly opposite her, only the narrow little desktop between them. This close, he could smell her. Soap, he thought, crisp and clean. And something faintly like rosemary that washed through him like heat. Better still, he could see the way her pulse went mad in the crook of her neck. "After all, what do you have if not your word? Your virtue?" He put enough emphasis on that last word that she cringed. "I understand that is a requirement for the charity you enjoy here. Your uncle has always been very clear on that score, has he not?"

She flushed again, harder this time. And Atlas shouldn't have been fascinated at the sight. He told himself it was nothing more than the vestiges of his prison time, making him find a female, any female, attractive. It wasn't personal.

Because it couldn't be personal. There was too much work to do.

"My uncle has never been anything but kind to me," she said in a low, intense voice, though there was a flicker in her gaze that made him wonder if she believed her own words.

"I know he requires you to believe it."

Another deep, red flash. "I understand that you're the last person in the world who could think kindly of the family. Any of them. And I don't blame you for that."

"I imagine I should view that as a kind of progress, that I am permitted my own bitterness. That it is no longer considered a part and parcel of my guilt, as if remorse for a crime I didn't commit might make me a better man."

Atlas regarded her stonily as she jerked a bit at that, though something in him...eased, almost. He'd spent all those years fuming, seething, plotting. He'd discarded more byzantine, labyrinthine plots than he cared to recall. That was what life in prison did to a man. It was fertile ground for grudges, the deeper, the better. But he'd never been entirely sure he'd get the opportunity to put all of this into motion.

"I won't lie to you, Lexi. I expected this to be harder."

"Your return?"

He watched, fascinated despite himself, as she pressed her lips together. As if they were dry. Or she was nervous. And Atlas was a man who had gone without female companionship for longer than he ever would have believed possible, before. No matter what else happened, he was still a man.

He could think of several ways to wet those lips.

But that was getting ahead of himself.

"I don't expect you to believe this," Lexi was saying with an intense earnestness that made him feel almost... restless. "But everyone feels terrible. My uncle. My cousins. All of us. Me especially. If I could change what happened, you have to believe I would."

"You're right," Atlas murmured. He waited for that faint bit of hope to kindle in her gaze, because he was nothing if not the monster they'd made him. "I don't believe it."

And really, she was too easy. He could read her too well. He saw the way she drooped, then collected herself. He watched her straighten again, then twist her hands together again. Harder this time.

"I know why you came here," she said after a moment. Quietly. "I expect your hatred, Atlas. I know I earned it."

"Aren't you the perfect little martyr?" When she shook a bit at that, he felt his mouth curve. "But it's not going to be that easy, Lexi. Nothing about this is going to be easy at all. If you come to a place of peace with that now, perhaps you will find this all less distressing." He shrugged. "Or perhaps not."

She looked panicked, but to her credit, she didn't move. She didn't swoon or scream or do any of the things Philippa would have done. No tantrums, no drama.

But then, Lexi had never been about theatrics.

That was precisely why she'd been such an effective witness for the prosecution, all starchy and matter-of-fact until she'd turned the knife in him, one glassy-eyed half sob at a time.

And what was wrong with him that he was tempted to forget that? For even a moment? He felt no connection to this woman. He couldn't. She was a pawn, nothing more.

It irritated him that he seemed to need reminding of that fact.

"What exactly is to come?" she asked, her voice hardly more than a breath and her eyes much too big in her face.

"I'm so glad you asked." He stood where he was, watching her. Studying her. Then he crooked a finger, and liked it a little too much when she jolted, as if he'd shot her through with lightning when he wasn't even touching her. Yet. "Come here."

She swayed on her feet and he was bastard enough to enjoy it. Hell, he more than enjoyed it. He figured it was as close as Lexi ever got to a full-on faint, and it was only a drop in the bucket next to the pain he owed her.

She swallowed, hard. He watched her throat move and

braced himself for a spate of complaints. Or excuses. Anything to avoid what was coming.

But she didn't say anything. She didn't argue or dawdle. She straightened that blouse of hers that was already precise to a near military level, and then she stepped out from behind her desk.

"Closer," Atlas ordered her when she only rounded the desk and stopped, leaving several feet between them.

Another hard, audible swallow. He could see her terror beat in her neck. He could see the flushed state of her skin. He could see fear and apprehension in her gaze, and the truth was, it was better than he'd imagined.

And God knew, he'd imagined this moment again and again and again. He'd imagined it so many times it was as if it had already happened. As if it was set in stone and made memory and prophecy at once.

She took one step. Then another.

"Here," Atlas said, gruff and cruel. And nodded his head to a spot on the floor about one inch in front of him.

And she surprised him yet again. There was no denying the uneasiness in her gaze, her expression. But she didn't carry on about it. She simply stepped forward, putting herself exactly where he'd indicated she should go.

Then he got to watch her tip her head back, way back, so she could hold his gaze with hers. And they could both spend a little moment or two recalling how much bigger and taller and more dangerous he was than she could ever dream of becoming.

He, at least, enjoyed the hell out of it.

"I think we can both agree that you owe me, can we not?" he asked.

It wasn't really a question. He didn't think she would confuse it for one, and he wasn't disappointed.

Her nod was jerky. "I wish I could change the past, but I can't."

"Indeed, you cannot. You cannot change one moment of the past eleven years."

"Atlas…"

He ignored her. "Your uncle has invited me to dinner tonight up at the manor house," he told her. "Perhaps you already know this."

"I know that was his intention, yes."

"Your uncle believes that breaking bread with me rather than squabbling in a boardroom or court of law will make this all go away." He could tell exactly how cruel his smile was by the way her brown eyes widened at the sight of it. "It won't."

"I don't think anyone expects any of this to go away."

"Wonderful. Then no one will be surprised by anything that happens now, I'm sure."

"Atlas. Please. No one meant to hurt you. You have to believe that."

It was an impassioned plea. He thought she even believed it. But he only shook his head at her.

"Let me tell you what I believe, Lexi. I believe that you were a teenager. That you saw something you didn't understand and put a spin on it that made sense to you. On some level, I don't even blame you for it. You were little more than a child, and of all the vultures and liars in this family, Philippa was at least the most genuine. In that I suspect she actually liked you."

She sucked in a breath, ragged and sharp at once. "They're my family. They all like me."

But he doubted even she thought that sounded convincing.

His mouth twisted into something as hard as it was sardonic. "Tell yourself those lies if you must. I cannot stop you. But do not tell them to me."

"You have a harsh view of the Worth family. I understand it and you have every right to it, but that doesn't mean I'm going to agree with you. *I* don't hate them the way you do."

He laughed at that. "The thing is, Lexi, your uncle was not a teenager. He was not confused. He knew exactly what he was doing, and you should ask yourself why he was so eager to do it."

"My uncle has never been anything but kind—"

"At the very least, Lexi, you must ask yourself why, when your uncle knew full well that I could not have killed his daughter, he pretended to think otherwise." Her breath sounded strangled, and he pushed on. "Your cousins, I think we can both agree, are varying degrees of useless. They believe whatever is most convenient and likely to fill their coffers. But you should know better. Is it that you don't—or that you won't?"

She seemed to struggle where she stood, and he let her.

"If you hate them all so much—if you hate *us* so much—I don't know what you're doing here." Her hands were no longer clenched in front of her. Instead, she'd curled them into fists at her sides. "You can go anywhere in the world, Atlas. Why return to a place that caused you so much pain?"

"Because I intend to cause pain in turn," Atlas told her, his voice hard. And he held her gaze in the same way, as if the look he was directing her way was a blow.

Good. It was.

"Surely there's been enough pain…" she whispered.

"You will be at that dinner tonight."

"I wasn't invited."

"I'm aware. Doesn't it fascinate you that while they

were happy to trot you out as a witness for the prosecution, they are less interested in having you attend my glorious return?"

"It's not that they're not interested, it's that I'm not the same as the rest of them. I don't have an interest in the estate's trust, for one thing."

"Though of all the Worth family blood relations, you are the only one who actually works for the trust. Does that not strike you as odd?"

She blinked and he thought he'd hit upon a sore spot. "Whether I do or don't doesn't matter. This is how things work here and everyone is perfectly happy with that. Except you, apparently. And I still wasn't asked to join your reunion dinner."

"I'm inviting you," he said, and watched her as she didn't react to that. As she very deliberately didn't react to that. "I told your uncle that I expected the entire family to be at that table and he's not inclined to cross me. Not this soon. Not while paparazzi still follow me around, desperate to record my every utterance."

"I don't know why you'd want me there. Surely you need to have a conversation with Uncle Richard, and my cousins, to discuss what is to become—"

"The first thing you need to learn, Lexi, is that I run this show." Atlas smiled at her, all fangs. "I will tell you when to speak and what to say, and if I do not, your job is to remain silent. After all, we both know you're very good at that, don't we?"

She went pale. "I don't know what you mean."

"I think you do. You've spent your entire life learning how to blend in with the scenery here." He raised his brows. "Do that."

She didn't like that. He could see it in the way her jaw moved, but she didn't rail at him the way he'd expected she might. Atlas was certain there was fire in her—temper and turmoil—but she never let it loose. Not even here, now, when it could be chalked up to the drama of this reunion.

"Whether I blend or don't blend," she said very carefully, as if she was weighing each word, "what does that have to do with you?"

He was far more comfortable with this part than with the unexpected perfection of the turn of her cheek. That he even noticed such a thing was a distraction and he couldn't afford distractions. Not now.

"At this dinner, I expect your uncle to offer me compensation for my years in prison. Money. A job. Whatever. It won't be enough."

"Can anything be enough?"

"I'm glad you asked. No."

"Then what do you hope—"

"I spent years trying to decide what would best serve my needs and also be the least palatable to your uncle," Atlas told her softly, in the tone that had kept more than one cell mate at bay. "And I could only think of one thing. I will reclaim my position, of course. I will take all the money that is owed me and then some. I will once again have all the things I worked so hard to achieve before they were stripped from me. But that will not return a decade of my life, will it?"

"Nothing will."

"Nothing," he agreed. "So you see, I have no choice but to make certain that this can never happen to me again. I will not be your uncle's patsy. I will not be a target. I will be something much, much worse." He smiled wider at that, dark and grim. "Family."

She didn't understand. He could see the confusion on her face, and like everything else about this meeting, it pleased him. Because he had never been a good man, he'd

only ever been an ambitious one. He'd fought his way out
of the slums with absolutely no help from anyone because
he'd refused to accept that he should stay there. While Lexi
had been coltish and silly at eighteen, Atlas had been focused. Determined.

There had never been another option.

He'd taken over his first company when he'd been barely
twenty and turned it into a global contender. He'd gone
from that to a boutique hotel chain in Europe that had
been on the verge of collapse and had turned all seven
locations into paragons of luxury, destinations in and of
themselves, and in so doing had made himself the most
sought after businessman in the world. The transformation
of Worth Manor and its grounds from tottery old heap of
family stones into a recreational destination in London, a
city packed with such things, had been supposed to send
him straight into the stratosphere.

Instead, he'd gone to prison. And he'd spent the past
eleven years learning that really, all he truly was beneath
all of that was furious.

As if *furious* was in his bones. As if *furious* was who
he was and ever would be.

Atlas was fine with that.

"I don't know what you're talking about," Lexi said,
and he had the sense she was fighting to remain calm. He
hoped it was a struggle.

"Your uncle will offer me a great many things tonight,"
Atlas told her, because he knew the old man. He knew exactly how this would go. He was depending on Richard
Xavier Worth being exactly who he'd always been. That
was the trouble with doing what Richard had done to a
man like Atlas, who had worked for him. Atlas had studied his boss. Richard should have taken better care to do

the same to the man he'd sent to prison. "And I will take them all. Then I will take one more thing. You."

He supposed it was a measure of her confusion that she only blinked at him. "Me?"

"Has it never occurred to you to wonder why it is your uncle goes to such great lengths to hide you away?" he asked, forcing himself to remain cool and calm even though this was the part he'd been looking forward to the most. "He treats you like the hired help, and you never think to question why that is, do you?"

"It's because that's essentially what I am," Lexi said briskly. If there was some emotion in her gaze, she blinked and it was gone. She even stood taller—likely because this was familiar ground for her. "And I'm grateful for that. I'm grateful for any shred of grace the Worths deign to throw my way. Because it's more than I ever would have gotten if my uncle had left me where I grew up."

He shouldn't have been surprised how deeply invested she was in that story. After all, he'd believed the old man, too, and he'd known better. How could a little girl have managed to hold out against a liar like Richard when Atlas had never seen any of this coming?

Not that he forgave her. Not even close.

"Yes, about that. Did you never think to question how it was your uncle found you so quickly?"

"I don't know what any of this has to do with what's happening here," Lexi burst out, with more emotion than he'd heard from her yet. She was more comfortable taking the blame than in spreading it around, Atlas thought. He needed to explore that—but only once he got his unruly fascination with the woman she'd become under control. "My mother walked away from this life. I feel lucky every single day that my uncle decided that just because he disowned her, that didn't mean he needed to write me off, too."

But again, despite the words she used, Atlas was certain he saw a hint of something else on her face. As if she wasn't as meekly grateful and humbly subservient as she acted.

"Because your uncle is nothing if not emotional," he said derisively, hoping that might tease Lexi's real thoughts out. "Family first, that's what he's known for."

She flushed at his harshly ironic tone. "He's a little reserved, yes, but—"

"Your uncle never had the power to disown your mother, Lexi," Atlas said, and even though he'd been leading up to this from the start, since before he'd stepped outside his cell, he made himself sound impatient. Gruff and dark, because he knew it got to her.

And so it did. She squirmed.

"Do you understand what I'm saying to you?" he asked when she made no reply. "You are as much a Worth family heiress as Philippa was. All your mother's money was held from her and is now yours. With interest."

"That's not possible," she said, almost dully. Almost as if she couldn't entirely process what he was saying.

"Of course, because your mother was such a disaster, there's a little clause in your trust. If your uncle does not approve of the man you marry, you will never see a penny of your fortune. And if you never marry, he will continue to handle that fortune as he sees fit, lest you be drawn into a marriage like your parents' at some point in the future."

"My…" She shook her head, her gaze blank. He thought perhaps she was shocked. "I don't have a fortune."

"But you see, you do. You always have." Atlas reached over and took her chin in his fingers before he knew he meant to move at all, much less touch her. He told himself the bolt of sensation that seared through him at so innocuous a touch was about his years in prison, not her. He needed a woman. Any woman. He told himself it had nothing to do with *this* woman, particularly. But he also didn't let go. "And I want it."

"You want...?"

"You, Lexi." Atlas smiled. Not at all nicely. "I want you. When your uncle asks what else he can give me, that is what I will tell him. That I intend to marry you. And that he will give his enthusiastic blessing to the match or live to regret it."

"None of this... I'm not..." Her chin trembled in his grip. "He won't do that. For any number of reasons."

"He will," Atlas said, stone and certainty, and furious all the way through. "Because if he does not, I will burn this place, and this family, straight down to the ground, Lexi. And better yet—I'll enjoy it."

CHAPTER THREE

LEXI WAS THE only one who had not dressed for dinner, which had the immediate effect of making her feel like a scullery maid. She tried to suck that in and bury it beneath her usual unflappably serene expression—the one she'd practiced in the mirror for years when she was younger—but as she stood in the family drawing room before dinner in her wilted office clothes while all around her swanned her cousins in the typical Worth family finery, she found it grated.

Or maybe it was that everything grated, suddenly, and her clothes were just a symptom.

She had no idea where the rest of her afternoon had gone.

Atlas had left the carriage house and she'd stood where he left her for a long, long time, as if she'd forgotten how to move. At some point she remembered, because she'd moved to the window near the polished stones she'd collected during the one beach holiday her parents had ever taken her on, and that was where she found herself as twilight began to fall over the estate. It was like a fugue state, and it left her no time to return to her flat, change into one of her few more formal dresses and then get back in time for dinner.

Maybe there was a part of her that had wanted it that

way, she'd thought as she'd walked the twenty minutes
across the park toward the manor house. Maybe something in her *wanted* to walk into one of Worth Manor's
famous formal dinners dressed like an office drone, every
inch of her the obviously poor relation she'd been to these
people since Uncle Richard had come to collect her at
eight years old.

Except…if what Atlas had said to her was true, she'd
never been the poor relation at all.

Did they all know it? Were they all a part of this, or did
they all believe the same story Lexi always had?

Lexi couldn't let herself think about it too closely. It was
too much to pile on top of the lingering effects of Philippa's
murder and the greater worry of Atlas's return. The fact
that Atlas had gotten out of prison in the first place felt
like entirely too much to handle, if she was honest. Much
less that he'd come straight for her. The things he'd thrown
out so cavalierly, as if they were simple little facts like the
color of the walls instead of literally life-altering—well.
How could she possibly process any of that? It was too
much. *He* was too much.

Not to mention the things he'd said to her. Much less
threatened.

"What are you doing here?" her cousin Harry asked
her when she settled herself on the farthest settee in the
drawing room, where she'd assumed she was least likely
to attract notice or offend anyone with her presence. He
was a tad too provoking for her tastes, but that was Harry.
Red of face and shockingly ginger of hair, but nothing so
attractive as the redheaded prince who shared his name.
This Harry was always drunk and bitter. "Do you have
something for Father to sign?"

And Lexi felt it then. That twisted, tangled, knotted
thing inside her that she'd worked so hard all these years

to ignore. To keep tucked away so nobody could possibly suspect it was lurking in there, the dark and forever angry little part of her that had always found the compulsory gratitude that was expected of her a little too hard to produce on cue.

Especially when she was treated like the lowliest member of the staff instead of family.

"I was invited," she said, perhaps more coldly than necessary.

She didn't say by whom. If Harry was surprised by that, or her chilly tone, he buried it in his back-to-back pre-dinner cocktails the way he always did. And by the time the whole of the family was gathered in the drawing room, Harry was well on his way to being entirely drunk. And the reckless way he ran his mouth when intoxicated was far more interesting to concentrate on than the reason everyone was standing there, speaking to each other in quietly appalled, obviously anxious tones.

As if that would make any difference. As if the quietness would save them, somehow, when Lexi felt certain that Atlas wouldn't care if they screamed and shouted. In fact, he might prefer it that way.

He, of course, was late.

"You'd think the one thing a person might learn in prison was how to be on time," her cousin Gerard muttered. His wife, the self-satisfied Lady Susan—who never missed an opportunity to flaunt the fact that she was both titled and had provided Gerard with an heir and two spares to cement her position in the family forever—tittered.

Lexi stayed where she was, on the settee tucked beneath the far window. She felt different, somehow, than she normally did when she found herself in the middle of the Worth family. As if the fact that Atlas was innocent had changed something in her, too.

Or as if the things he'd said to her today had made it impossible for her to view anything in the way she had before. As if he'd torn the veil from her eyes without her consent and it didn't matter, anyway, because there was no going back now that she could *see*. Maybe that was why she found herself studying these people, *her family*, whom she'd spent most of her life wanting desperately to include her.

For twenty years now, all she'd wanted was to feel as if she was a part of this. Of them. And the truth was that she never had.

In those twenty years, only Philippa had ever treated Lexi as if she was something more than a charity case. Only Philippa had ever acted as if she cared—and that had been such a long time ago it was almost as if Lexi had made it up. Dreamed it, perhaps, a decade back when she'd still been so young and hopeful.

Only Philippa—and occasionally, back in those gleaming days before anything bad had happened, Atlas.

Lexi didn't want to think about what Atlas had said to her earlier. And worse, if what he'd said was true, what that meant about everything she'd believed about her life all these years. She didn't want to consider all the implications—but she couldn't quite seem to help herself.

She concentrated on her uncle. Richard looked like exactly who he was and always had been. A very wealthy man indeed, whose consequence stretched back several centuries to a time when the first Worth merchants had emerged from the unwashed masses and dared to claim a place in British society. He was inordinately proud of the fact he still had a full head of leonine white hair and stood a bit above six feet. He ran a religious few miles every morning and swore by an evening constitutional around the grounds to digest his dinner. He was a careful man, Lexi would have said, despite his vanity—or perhaps because of it. He considered his every move deeply and dispassionately.

If he was disconcerted by Atlas's return, he was the only one who didn't show it. Richard stood in one of his quietly masterful suits at the mantel over the crackling fire. He hardly touched the drink he held. That he was irritated with Harry's drunkenness was evident only in the faintest curl of his austere lips. That he had never had any particular use for Lady Susan was equally evident in the way he failed to look at her directly, no matter how she tittered and made a show of herself.

Lexi thought Gerard was Richard's favorite, but tonight she wondered if that was true—or if Gerard was simply the only one who didn't inspire his father to visibly fight the urge to roll his eyes. She tried to remember how he'd treated Philippa, but that had been so long ago. And Lexi had been so young and easily embarrassed herself that it was hard to remember what had really happened and what was simply her own potential overreaction to things.

Before tonight, Lexi had never considered the fact that her uncle's complete lack of expression when he looked at her was a kind of blessing. It was neutral, anyway. She wondered if that put her higher in his estimation than Harry—or at least, drunken Harry. Or Lady Susan and her tittering.

Then again, perhaps his neutral expression when he looked at her was simply because Richard Worth didn't stir himself to have visible reactions to anyone who wasn't a member of his nuclear family.

Damn Atlas for making all of that seem nefarious.

Lexi was the first to hear the footsteps in the hall. She sat a little straighter, her gaze on the door, but no one else seemed to hear anything. The footsteps drew closer.

Then closer still, that same dark-sounding tread that announced Atlas like the drums of war. It wasn't until he was right outside the door that all the Worths tensed, and Lexi couldn't tell if they'd been pretending not to hear him earlier or if they'd truly been oblivious. Either way, the drawing room fell silent.

And this time, when Atlas pushed through the door, he was smiling.

"How delightful," Atlas murmured, stopping in the doorway again, as if he knew exactly what kind of entrance he made and wanted to make sure they gazed at him there—not in handcuffs, not in a courtroom, not on a television screen from across the sea—for as long as possible. "All together again, just as I asked."

"Welcome home, Atlas," Uncle Richard said, after only the faintest pause. He even lifted his glass.

Atlas's smile seemed to get darker. Sharper. He moved farther into the tidy little drawing room decked out in its Victorian finery, his black glare sweeping from one wall to the next, then back. Lexi found herself holding her breath while her pulse went wild—and hated herself for her own reaction.

It was the same reaction she'd always had to him. Only tonight it was worse.

"And what a home it is," Atlas was saying in that same too-dark approximation of joviality. "Imagine my delirious joy to find that every single improvement I suggested during my tenure as CEO has been implemented. Every. Single. One. I took a long tour of the house and grounds today, and it warms my convict heart. It truly does. What a visionary I was. Feel free to applaud at will."

"Listen, you—" Harry started, all red and snarly, but he subsided with a single harsh look from his father.

"There's no need for all this menacing scenery-chewing, surely," Uncle Richard said into the tense silence, his voice bland. Much blander than the cold gleam in his eyes. "We're all quite aware of the role you played in... well, everything."

"To clarify, do you mean the fantasy evil villain role you cast me in that landed me in jail?" Atlas asked with soft menace. "Or are you referring to the actual reality of what I did here that lacked any murderous intent but *did* manage to transform the place from a crumbling old mausoleum into...all this?"

Lexi saw the muscles leap in her uncle's cheek and knew he was clenching his jaw. Just as she was clenching hers. She made herself relax. A little.

"No one can change the past," Uncle Richard said in a gravelly sort of way, somber and serious. "We can only move forward, I'm afraid."

Atlas accepted a drink from the wide-eyed footman, but Lexi noticed he didn't take a sip of it. He only played with it in his hand, swirling the amber liquid this way, then that, as if he was enjoying a relaxing evening surrounded by loved ones.

"To the future," he said in that same mild tone with its darker edge, then lifted his tumbler toward the light.

It was the most awkward toast in history. The room was silent, but filled with tension. So much tension Lexi was half-afraid it would choke them all where they stood.

But no. Dutifully, helplessly, everyone lifted their glasses. Even Harry, though he still wore that same dark scowl on his face.

Even Lexi, though she knew better.

Atlas didn't say another word. He simply stood there a scant inch or two in front of the door—almost as if he was blocking it. It felt as if he was. He was dark and commanding and entirely too enigmatic, especially when all he did was swirl his drink around and let his black, fulminating gaze land on whomever he chose.

As if he was taking mental notes, none of them flattering, and committing them to memory where he stood.

"I feel a bit like an animal in a zoo, really," Lady Susan said with a little sniff after a few moments of this intense scrutiny dragged on by, but subsided when Gerard frowned at her.

Atlas stared at her a little harder after that, likely to make Lady Susan even more uncomfortable. And all Lexi could think was *thank God he isn't watching* me *like that*.

Though what would it matter if he was? She reminded herself—with some force—that she'd handled Atlas all on her own earlier. And she'd survived just fine.

Perfectly fine, she assured herself. Maybe a little too sharply. She was still in one piece, anyway.

When they were finally called into dinner, it came as a relief.

Atlas walked ahead, bold and sure, as if this was his house and the rest of them nothing more than uninvited guests. Was Lexi the only one who wondered if that was his endgame? Gerard and Lady Susan trailed behind him, Harry on their heels, more as if they were worried Atlas might make off with the silver than because they were in any hurry to break bread with the man—or concerned about what he might take from them.

Uncle Richard hung back and took Lexi's arm, and there was no reason that should have made her pulse racket around inside her, making her feel faintly sick. Her uncle might not have been the warmest man alive, but he'd never been unkind to her.

Or not too unkind, anyway.

It was Atlas's poison in her head, that was all. She tried to shake it off.

"I understand you received a visitor this afternoon," Richard said as he led Lexi down the hall toward the family dining room, which was considered more intimate and cozy than the formal dining hall below, though it could seat twenty with ease.

"Yes." She snuck a look at her uncle, then returned her gaze to the floor in front of her. "As you can imagine, he had some hard things to say to me about my testimony. I imagine he's been saving them up all this time."

Uncle Richard did not look down the length of the dining room as they entered. He didn't have to. Just as Lexi didn't have to look up from her contemplation of the floor to know exactly where Atlas was. She could feel his black glare, burning into her from the far end of the elegant chamber, making her worry she might burst into flame in another moment.

"You must tell me if he becomes abusive," Richard said in a voice that wasn't exactly affectionate. But that wasn't his style, she reminded herself. Not everything was a conspiracy, no matter what Atlas thought. "That will not be tolerated."

Lexi smiled as politely as she could but inside, everything seemed to slosh this way and that, like a kind of internal riot. She didn't know what her uncle thought he could possibly do to Atlas. This was Atlas's show, as he'd said himself in the carriage house.

But the worst part was she knew that even this morning, just hours ago, she would have believed that her uncle said such a thing to her out of concern. It would have warmed her. She would have taken it as some kind of sign that he really did view her as family after all.

Tonight she felt nothing but manipulated.

She wondered how he knew that Atlas had stopped by to see her. Had the secretary reported back? Was he having Atlas followed? Did he keep tabs on Lexi herself? She hated that all these questions were cluttering up her head. She hated that she couldn't simply walk into dinner with the closest thing she'd ever had to a father and be happy with it.

"Did you know he was innocent?" she asked her uncle quietly.

And was instantly horrified that she'd dared. She raised her gaze to his, slowly, aware that she'd flushed hot in some combination of embarrassment and worry that she'd stepped over a line.

But Uncle Richard didn't react. He only stared back at her, his expression as neutral as it ever was. "What an extraordinary question. Is that what he told you?"

She didn't know why she didn't just nod. "No."

"You wondered such a thing yourself, then?" Her uncle smoothed the front of his jacket. "After all this time?"

"No one ever spoke of it," Lexi said in an undertone, lest the entire room start paying attention to this quiet little exchange. "We never discussed that night once the trial ended."

"There hardly seemed to be a need." Uncle Richard peered at her in a way she didn't like. At all. "You seem unwell, Lexi. Perhaps all of this is a bit too much for you. Shall I call you a car?"

She didn't know which was worse. That she knew, without a shred of doubt, that her uncle was deliberately trying to remove her from this dinner. Or that the fact he was doing such a thing meant Atlas was likely correct in everything he'd told her. Or that this was the first time she could recall her uncle offering her a pleasant car ride home rather than her usual walk and bus ride, which might have warmed her heart before.

Tonight it made her even more uneasy.

She smiled at him as he walked her to her seat.

"You're lovely to look out for me," she said, and maybe she was watching her uncle too closely. Maybe that was why she saw the way his eyes narrowed, as if he knew full well she didn't believe him. "I think we're all a bit raw."

Uncle Richard only made a low, noncommittal sort of noise at that. He pulled out her chair in another show of courtesy that startled her. She sat before she could think twice about it and regretted it when she realized her uncle had put her directly across from Atlas. She would have protested if she could think of a way to do it without revealing herself.

Of course you would have, something in her jeered. *You with all your backbone.*

She might not have been the most outspoken person alive, it was true. That had been Philippa, and any fantasies Lexi might have had to follow her lead had died when she had. Still, Lexi didn't want anyone to know *how much* Atlas got to her. She didn't want anyone to connect any of those dots. She was certain that it would kill her if they did. She would simply ignore him, she decided, and dedicate herself to enjoying the meal, which was sure to be exquisite—because Uncle Richard demanded nothing less. Dinner was one of the only things she'd missed in these years of living outside the manor house.

But what little appetite she might have had was put off by the man who lounged there across from her, making no effort whatsoever to hide that insolent, darkly amused expression on his face as he looked around the table at the people he'd called here tonight to dance to his tune.

"Such a warm, welcoming gathering of beloved family and friends," he drawled, playing it up. "What a glorious homecoming, I think we can all agree."

And a glance around the table told Lexi that everyone felt as tortured as she did.

Still, everything was scrupulously polite. At first.

The house staff began serving starters as Uncle Richard and Gerard spoke in the broadest generalities about the estate. The news. That most British of topics, the weather. From time to time, Lady Susan would interject her own comment or reaction, or even the odd titter. Harry didn't say a word, but a glance at his surly grimace and Lexi thought that was likely for the best. For her part, she picked at her first course, just enough to look as if she was eating while actually doing little more than moving the food around on her plate.

She couldn't have even said what it was. It all tasted like ash in her mouth.

Across from her, Atlas was making no attempt whatsoever to join in the usual, blandly inoffensive dinner patter all around him.

He didn't even pretend to eat.

He simply sat there, his legs thrust out before him as he leaned back in his chair, one hand on the table before him, drumming out a little rhythm next to his cutlery.

Tap-tap. Tap-tap.

There was no reason whatsoever that Lexi should feel that as if he was using a hammer and a chisel against the side of her own poor head.

Except for the fact that Atlas wasn't looking at her uncle. Nor her cousins. He kept that black gaze of his trained directly on Lexi, that hint of a sardonic curve in the corner of his lethal mouth.

And she tried. She tried her very best to lie to herself. She told herself that he had only been throwing his weight around in her office earlier, which was only to be expected after his ordeal. That he couldn't possibly mean the things that he'd said to her, because it was all so ridiculous.

Her uncle was quiet and reserved and, if she was being uncharitable, perhaps too concerned with what he perceived as his legacy. What he was not was a manipulative bastard straight out of a Dickens novel, murderous and cruel. Atlas was angry, that was all.

And as much as Lexi understood that and more, felt terrible for her part in this tragedy, she certainly didn't need to make it easy for him to play his little power games.

She sat straighter in her chair. She crossed her ankles beneath her, fought to keep her expression serene and forced herself to join in the conversation.

Anything to prove he doesn't get to you, that same little voice murmured inside her.

It wasn't until the main course had been served in another stretch of painfully tense silence that Atlas spoke again.

"There's no need to dance around the elephant in the room," he said, cutting into the desultory sort of conversation Gerard and Uncle Richard were having about the footie, making Lexi wonder if football bored Atlas as thoroughly as it did her. "Don't you want to know what it is I want?"

"Compensation, presumably," Gerard said at once. He had his own head of leonine hair, though his was still sandy. And his skin tended toward the ruddy, especially when he was attempting to sound like the elder statesman he aspired to become. He nodded at Atlas as if they weren't more or less the same age. "That's understandable, of course."

"Compensation," Atlas echoed, still drumming his fingers against the table. "What a fascinating word. What do you imagine could possibly compensate me for a decade of my life lost? For a reputation destroyed? For year after year in a foreign cage?"

"I imagine you have a number in your head already," Uncle Richard said. Much too coolly, Lexi thought, then despaired of herself for siding with Atlas instead of these people who'd cared for her all this time, however indifferently. "No need for all the suspense."

"Ah, Richard," Atlas murmured, as if he was amused, when Lexi felt certain he was not. "There are some things that money can't buy."

"I have never found that to be the case," Uncle Richard replied. He inclined his head. "Especially where ambitious young men are concerned."

Lexi put down her fork, certain that she might be sick. And yet wasn't.

"If I wanted money," Atlas said softly—too softly— after a beat, "I would simply sue. But I have no plans to do so at present. That could change, of course."

"A court of law found you guilty, Atlas," Harry interjected, sounding even drunker and more furious than before. "Are you planning to sue them, too? Or is it only us who must pay?"

Lexi held her breath.

But Atlas only laughed.

CHAPTER FOUR

ATLAS'S LAUGHTER FILLED the room, dark and ruthless.

Confronting and derisive at once, like a black stain Lexi worried she'd never wash out. She couldn't seem to pull in a full breath. Or much of any breath at all, come to that. Her eyes were too full and she was *this close* to trembling—or maybe she already was, but was too caught in that awful laughter to be able to tell.

"I'm sure the guilty verdict was all a coincidence," Atlas said softly, while the remains of that black stain still spun through the room, turning everything as dark as the look on his face. "Or a miscarriage of justice you all happened to applaud as real. Still, nothing delights me more than to be welcomed back, with such love and genuine affection, into the heart of this, my second family."

"Family…?" Harry sputtered. But he was sufficiently intoxicated by now that he only rolled his eyes when both Gerard and his father glared at him. "You were a hired hand, man. A glorified groundskeeper, at best. You might want to consider getting over yourself."

"This must be awkward for you," Atlas murmured, sounding something like apologetic when the look in his black eyes clearly indicated he was sorry about nothing. Not one thing. "Your father encouraged me to think of myself as another one of his sons from the day I arrived."

Atlas smiled as if he was being helpful, when Lexi had no doubt he was fully aware that he was not. At all. "Though I was perhaps more useful to him and this property than his actual sons."

Harry made as if to rise up from his chair, but stopped himself when Uncle Richard lifted his hand.

Lexi heard a ragged sound and realized it was her own harsh breathing. She tried to choke it back, with minimal success. But realized it hardly mattered as no one was paying particular attention to her. Not when Atlas was commanding center stage.

"I understand you feel the need to spill blood, but that's hardly productive, is it?" Uncle Richard asked.

He sounded eminently reasonable. Lexi had no idea why it put her back up.

Atlas seemed to sprawl even more in his chair. "I can't imagine why you think productivity interests me at all."

"What do you want, then?" Gerard gritted out, not sounding reasonable in the least.

Atlas was leaning as far back in his chair as it was possible to go without toppling over, and Lexi couldn't get past the notion that he was enjoying himself. That this was fun for him, somehow. Or at least that this was exactly what he'd had planned. This discomfort. This eternal awkwardness.

"We believed what we were told, Atlas," Richard said coolly. "What the police and prosecutors told us. I hope you haven't forgotten that Philippa is still lost to us, no matter what you feel you've suffered."

"I never forget that." Atlas's voice was a sharp slap. It seemed to rocket around the table, careening off every member of the family like a vicious ricochet. "I spent ten years in an American prison wondering what her actual killer was doing while I sat there, shouldering the blame."

"Just tell us what you want," Gerard burst out then, even grittier than before.

"As apologies go," Atlas observed, almost idly, "this one is rather lacking."

"I made it clear that I was happy to meet with you at any time you liked," Uncle Richard said smoothly. Maybe too smoothly for Lexi's taste. "I thought a dinner would make this inevitably awkward meeting a little easier for everyone concerned."

"You thought it would keep this meeting private," Atlas corrected him softly. "I doubt very much that you were worried about making it *easy*. Especially not for me."

"I take responsibility for not thinking it through. That was my mistake." Uncle Richard sighed heavily, his gaze on Atlas looking something like kind. But Lexi found she didn't believe that, either. "I didn't realize you were quite this bitter."

"I think you'll find that most falsely imprisoned people are rather bitter," Atlas replied, and this time he sounded very nearly merry, which made it all the more menacing. "And whether we meet in my solicitors' offices or aim phony smiles at each other across this table makes no difference to me. I am not the one who is emotional tonight. Or drunk. This is all going exactly the way that I thought it would." He lifted his glass again, lazy and mocking. "I congratulate you all on remaining entirely predictable."

Lexi flushed hot at that, as if those words had been directed at her alone. As if he was accusing her directly with that searing black gaze of his and that slight, sardonic twist to his impossibly cruel, still remarkably beautiful, lips.

"I'm not going to sit here and let you threaten me or anyone else," Harry blustered, and he suddenly sounded a good deal less intoxicated than he had before. "The fact is, you were too big for your britches then. Maybe you really didn't kill Philippa. Or more likely you were smart enough not to leave your prints."

"And yet not smart enough to keep myself out of prison."

"You're out of prison now." Harry glared back at Atlas, every inch of him stubborn and red. "Looks to me like you got away with it. You should be grateful. And I don't care what your panel of experts said, anyway."

"Because scientific facts are so tedious," Atlas murmured, as if he was agreeing with Harry when he clearly wasn't. "I understand."

"You can swan about giving interviews until you're blue in the face," Harry charged on. "I'm not going to pretend that I don't know exactly what happened."

"Never let it be said that stubborn ignorance cannot win out over even the most inarguable fact." Atlas smirked. "But I don't require that you like me or believe in me, Harry. In fact, I'm hoping you won't. Any of you," he clarified, and shifted that steady black glare of his from Harry to sweep it up and down the table again. "It will be so much less satisfying for me if any of you are at all happy, ever again."

"Because you want us to suffer," Lexi heard herself say, as if the words were torn from her own throat. And when everyone turned to look at her with varying degrees of shock, as if they'd forgotten she was sitting there, she didn't cringe and melt off beneath the table. Somehow, she kept right on talking. "That's why you came back. That's the only reason you came back."

Atlas let that curve in the corner of his mouth deepen.

"I'm sure that's not what he means," Lady Susan replied, sounding a little too sour for any tittering just then.

"That's exactly what I mean," Atlas corrected her. "Perhaps I'm being needlessly dramatic tonight. I don't mind if you achieve happiness *someday*. But I'd prefer it not be for at least the next eleven years. Just to make things equal. Balanced."

"This is absurd," Lady Susan said, scoffing, as if she was *just about* to collapse into scornful laughter but was somehow holding herself back.

"I don't mean you, Susan," Atlas assured her, a flash of heat in his voice that made Lexi recoil, though Susan didn't seem to hear it. "I don't think you're capable of happiness, forbidden or otherwise. Or you would be distinctly less tiresome."

In all the time that Lexi had known Susan, she'd never seen the other woman speechless. There was a first time for everything, however, and tonight was clearly that first time. Because Susan's mouth dropped open, but no sound emerged.

Something Lexi might have enjoyed under other circumstances. But Atlas settled back in his chair and smiled, not at all nicely, and Lexi assumed she wasn't the only one in the room who felt cold.

"So this is revenge," Uncle Richard said after another long moment of silence. "That's why you raced back here as soon as you were let out. Revenge."

"Is that meant to make me feel like a small, petty man?" Atlas asked with the same lazy inflection he kept using, that made Lexi feel entirely too…restless. "Are you attempting to shame me into forgetting what you did to me?" He waved a hand. "You'll soon realize that I feel no shame whatsoever."

"Listen, we're happy to do our part to help you adjust after all this unpleasantness," Gerard threw out there. "But you can't expect us to take responsibility for the jury's verdict. Besides, we're the ones who lost a family member."

"On the contrary, I expect you to take full responsibility," Atlas told him with a quiet ferocity. "But that's really the least of it. I also expect you to meet my demands. Every single one of them. And let's just get this out of the way up front, shall we? You won't like them."

Lexi didn't know which of her cousins made noise at that, but it didn't matter. Atlas was staring at Uncle Richard, who was staring back at him with an arrested look on his face. Or maybe he was just haunted.

The way they all were by the terrible things they couldn't change. The night that Philippa had died. The years that Atlas had lost. All of them trapped together in the same tight grip of loss and fear, rage and shame.

Maybe the truth was they were all responsible.

Lexi had no idea why she didn't open her mouth and say that.

"Go on, then." Richard squared his shoulders, ignoring the shocked looks he got from both his sons. "Make your demands, if you must."

Atlas's smile widened, which could only bode ill.

"It will be more *productive*—" and Lexi didn't think anyone in the room missed the way he emphasized that last word "—to consider this a restoration project. Not revenge, as such. If only so you can all feel better about it." His smile was a weapon, Lexi understood then. Sharp and lethal and he knew exactly how to wield it. "That's the important thing, of course. That's what guides me. That you all feel good about the situation."

Lexi was surprised she couldn't hear her uncle's teeth grind together from all the way at her end of the table, given the set to his jaw.

"He's enjoying this," Harry snarled then. He shoved back his chair, tossing his linen napkin in the vague direction of his plate, and didn't seem to notice when it fell to the floor. He was too busy standing there at his place at last, all bristling temper and obvious outrage. "He's loving every single minute."

"Wouldn't you?" Lexi asked.

In an exasperated tone she didn't know she had in her.

All eyes turned to her at that and she instantly wished the floor would swallow her up. She didn't even know where it had come from. She'd been sitting silently through Harry's various rampages and rants and complaints for as long as she could remember. The past twenty years, certainly. Since the day Uncle Richard had brought her home, sat her at this very table for a dinner just like this one and had done absolutely nothing when Harry had complained about "taking in strays."

And she'd had no idea she'd been holding on to that memory all this time.

"What did you just say?" Harry asked, sounding as shocked as he was belligerent, though the snarl he aimed down the table at Lexi was rather more the latter.

"Of course he's enjoying this," Lexi said, fighting to keep her tone even, and not happy that it was so much harder than it should have been. "If I had to sit in a prison cell for ten years, I'm certain that I, too, would come up with elaborate revenge plots and then enjoy seeing them to fruition." She eyed her cousin. "This is nothing more than an uncomfortable dinner for you, Harry. It's not a cell block you have to sit in for a decade while completely innocent of the charges against you."

The worst part wasn't the way her uncle regarded her then, with a kind of calculation that made her stomach turn. It wasn't Lady Susan's overly plucked brows creeping halfway up her forehead. It wasn't even the way her cousins scowled at her.

The worst part was that kick in her heart when her gaze clashed with Atlas's across the table. It took the wind right out of her. It reminded her exactly how foolish she'd always been where this man was concerned. It shot her straight back into the worst, most humiliating part of her teenage years here, trailing around like a lovesick puppy with big, obvious stars in her eyes, trying to spend as much time in Atlas's vicinity as possible.

It made her think that even though everything had changed, absolutely everything in her life that had ever mattered to her, some things remained exactly the same.

And most of all, it made her wonder why she'd done something so stupid as defend him when no one here was likely to hear her, anyway. All she'd done was call unwelcome attention to herself.

"I imagine this is why he visited you earlier, then," Uncle Richard said softly, and while his tone was perfectly friendly, the look in his eyes was frigid. Lexi had to fight off the urge to shiver. "He wanted an ally."

Lexi let out a small laugh at that, because she'd apparently lost all control over herself. "That's not what he wanted at all."

"I'm perfectly capable of telling you exactly what I want, in detail," Atlas interjected then. "Eager, even. Let's start with this. Since an apology has yet to be forthcoming, we'll move on to more practical concerns, shall we?"

"No one is going to apologize for something that wasn't their fault," Uncle Richard said. Though that cold gaze of his was still on Lexi.

"You and I have different definitions of fault, I think." Atlas shrugged. "It is of no matter tonight. But I do want my job back. My job and everything that went with it, that I worked so hard to build."

"Why on earth would you want to work for us again?" Gerard asked stiffly.

"And that's another thing," Atlas said, in that amused

way of his that made everything inside Lexi feel too tight. Too sharp. As if she was made of glass and was set to shatter. "I don't want to work for you. I'm not interested in being the hired help again. You people have a nasty habit of throwing the servants into the fire at a moment's notice. I think I'll pass on taking that fall again, thank you."

"But you just said…" Harry began, still standing there at his place as if he hadn't decided whether to flip the table or storm from the room.

"I will be CEO of the Worth Trust again," Atlas said mildly. "Believe that, if nothing else. Whether you choose to do the right thing and make that easy or force me to take back what is mine through the courts is of no matter to me. I will win either way."

She knew where he was going with this, and maybe that was why Lexi could do nothing but admire—grudgingly, she assured herself—the calm way he delivered all of this. One bomb after the next, keeping everyone off balance as he carefully set his trap. She'd spoken without thinking just then, but it was clear to her that Atlas did no such thing. That all of this was meticulously planned.

And that knowledge made her shudder, deep inside.

Because if it had all been planned—everything he was saying here, everything he'd said to her—that clearly meant this was only the tip of the iceberg.

And whatever else he had planned, she could assume he not only meant business, but also aimed to destroy all of them. One by one, until he felt adequately revenged for what had been done to him.

Maybe it wasn't such a surprise that she was first on that particular funeral pyre. And maybe she shouldn't have been so shocked that she was somewhat less churned up by that than she should have been. Because there was still that goggle-eyed teen inside her, she was ashamed to admit to herself, and she liked whatever attention this man gave her. Positive or negative. Even if she was nothing but a pawn in his revenge game.

How sad is that? asked that hard, little voice inside her. *You do so love a chance to make yourself a martyr, don't you?*

That didn't sit well with Lexi. But she suspected the reason it didn't was because it was true.

"But to be clear, I will not be working for the Worth family again," Atlas was saying. "As charming as that experience was, I intend to be a part of the family this time. No longer only in word, but deed and fact. One of those facts you dismiss so easily, Harry." He smiled again, and it was even worse than before. "Oh, happy day."

"What the bloody hell you talking about?" Harry cried, sounding a little too close to enraged.

Gerard was glaring. Lady Susan looked mystified and faintly nauseated. But Lexi noted that her uncle didn't look surprised at all. Or shocked. Or even the least bit confused.

He was watching Lexi, not Atlas.

As if he knew exactly where this was heading.

And much as she tried to deny it, as much as she *wanted* to deny it, Lexi understood with perfect clarity that if her uncle knew where Atlas was going with this, then somehow, that validated everything Atlas had told her. About her uncle. About this family.

About who Lexi really was.

Her stomach twisted into a painful knot, then dropped down to the floor at her feet.

Because she hadn't wanted to believe him. All that talk of fortunes and lies. All the things it would mean—like the bedsit she lived in and tried to count herself lucky to have, even though her paltry salary from her job here barely covered her rent. Like the way these people had treated her all these years, as if she was, at best, an inconvenience. A charity case and a burden.

Like the fact they'd all expected her to be grateful for the scraps of a life they'd thrown her way.

Of course she hadn't wanted to believe it. Who wanted to believe their entire life was a deliberate falsehood told to her by people who should have cared for her?

But Uncle Richard was watching *her,* not Atlas, and Lexi couldn't lie to herself the way she wanted to do. Not anymore.

"Congratulate me," Atlas invited everyone, and smiled around the table, all deep male satisfaction and something a great deal like triumph on his face. "I'm marrying your cousin."

"Our cousin?" Harry asked, as if he'd forgotten he had one.

"Lexi?" Gerard asked, in the same tone—remembering Lexi existed, perhaps, but baffled as to why that should matter.

"Why the hell would you do that?" Harry demanded. "Do you need a secretary?"

"How is that revenge?" Lady Susan asked. And then tittered, long and loud.

And Lexi told herself that there would be no benefit whatsoever to snatching up the knife beside her plate and stabbing her cousins to death, right here and now. All that would do was put her into the prison cell Atlas had just vacated.

But her fingers curled around the knife's handle, anyway.

"Thank you all," she said, because after twenty years of bowing, scraping silence, she apparently could no longer keep her mouth shut. "I appreciate the support." She swallowed, hard, but she wasn't done. She glared at Harry.

"And not that you care or have ever noticed, Harry, but I'm not a secretary. I'm in charge of all the estate programming and—"

"Let me make sure I understand what's happening here," Uncle Richard said quietly. Too quietly. And the way he was looking at Lexi made her skin crawl and more, made her forget whatever she was about to say. "You have accepted this proposal? Is that what took place this afternoon in the carriage house? This...engagement?"

Something sparked inside her at that word. *Engagement.* Almost as if...but she shoved that dangerous line of thought aside, because nothing here was hearts and flowers. Only a fool would think otherwise. And she wasn't fooled by the seeming pleasantness of the way her uncle had asked his questions.

She smiled. Stiffly. "Calling it an engagement suggests I had a choice in the matter."

"Of course you have a choice, Lexi," Atlas chimed in then. Almost warmly, really, which Lexi found unforgivable. "It's just that you won't like your other option. I can promise you that."

"Wonderful," Lexi said. She folded her hands in her lap and raised her brow at her uncle. "There you go. Have you ever heard of anything so romantic?"

"I don't understand this," Harry said impatiently. "Why would you marry Lexi? She's not even—"

He stopped himself before he went any further, but then, there was no need to go on. His meaning was clear.

And Lexi felt that knotted thing inside her grow all the more tangled as she stared across the table at Atlas.

Atlas, who had predicted this. Atlas, who'd known.

Atlas, who looked entertained.

Atlas who, she was sure, would only delight in it if he

had the slightest idea that the things she felt about him were so...complicated.

"I will marry Lexi," Atlas announced to the table, again, with more force behind his words this time, as if he was daring anyone to contradict it. "It will be a joyous, splendid occasion. All of you will fall all over yourselves to tell the papers about your deep, personal support for the union. *What a sweet and glorious end to a sad and tragic tale,* you'll say. *How wonderful that we can welcome Atlas into the family as the son we always believed he was.* You understand."

"I'm not saying any of that," Harry said with a laugh, and clearly felt sufficiently amused by that to take his seat again. "Prison made you delusional, clearly."

"I have not been Lexi's guardian in a decade," Uncle Richard said, in a tone Lexi couldn't read. Still, it made her stiffen. "It's not up to me to tell her who to marry, or even whether she should marry at all."

"This is not up for debate or discussion," Atlas said, in that mild way of his that made Lexi's toes ache so much she had to press them into the floor. Hard. "You will support this marriage, Richard. And in so doing, take your greedy little fingers off Lexi's fortune at last."

There was that word again. *Fortune.* Lexi still couldn't make sense of it, not applied to her.

But neither could anyone else in the room.

"Fortune?" Lady Susan asked, looking shocked. She frowned at her husband. "What fortune? Has he confused Lexi with Philippa?"

"Lexi has no bloody fortune," Harry chimed in. "Lexi lives off this family's charity, that's all."

"If by *charity* you mean a job that she's worked consistently and well since she was eighteen," Lexi heard herself say, which was so unlike her it should have toppled her from her chair. But it didn't, and she had the sneaking suspicion that had something to do with the way Atlas was looking at her. Not with approval, exactly. But as if he expected no less than this from her, which, somehow, made it easier. "Unlike other people at this table."

"What the hell is he talking about?" Gerard demanded of Uncle Richard, ignoring Lexi entirely, which was its own kind of obnoxious. And telling in its way, she thought.

But Uncle Richard was conspicuously silent.

"Oh, hasn't he told you?" Atlas asked, all innocence and lazy delight. "Your grandfather left the Worth estate and all of its income to both his children, divided equally." He nodded at Gerard and Harry as if they were idiots. "I mean your father and Lexi's mother, of course. When Yvonne died, her half of the Worth fortune—which was, I think you'll find, intact once your father stopped giving her money—was left entirely to Lexi."

"Yvonne was disowned when she married," Gerard snapped out. "Everyone knows that."

"Was she?" Atlas asked quietly. "Are you certain?"

Gerard's gaze swung back to his father, who continued to say nothing.

And there was something tight around Lexi's throat, making it hard to breathe. To do anything but sit there and spin wildly about in her seat, because everything she'd ever been told about this family and her place in it was a lie.

A deep, dark, entirely deliberate lie her uncle had told her since she was eight years old.

She was afraid that if she looked at Richard then she would…do something. Cry. Scream. Throw her knife his way.

Or worst of all, beg him to tell her why he'd treated her this way.

"Let me do the math for you, in case that's difficult after

so many years playing Oxbridge games. All of this—"
Atlas made a small gesture with one hand that seemed to
encompass everything. The dining room. The grand manor
house. The whole Worth estate. Possibly the entire world.
"—is half Lexi's. The rest of you—the three of you here
and all of Gerard's spawn, if my numbers are correct—get
to squabble with each other over whatever pieces remain of
Richard's half. Assuming he chooses to share it, of course."

"This can't be true," Harry said, letting out a stilted sort
of laugh that seemed to squat there on the table like something foul. "Father. Tell him this is madness."

Atlas nodded down the length of the table toward Uncle
Richard, who said nothing.

"When I marry Lexi—which will happen with some
haste so as to prevent any further unfortunate events, like
another murder charge—I will not only take control of the
Worth Trust, I'll also be a constant and eager help to my
wife as she comes to terms with her place here. Her right-
ful place, which is not that of an overworked office drone.
But as an heiress fully committed to taking control of her
lands and money at last."

And then Atlas sat there, marinating happily in the
stunned silence he'd created, if that look on his face was
any guide.

It was Lexi's heart that beat too fast. It was her breath
that failed to penetrate much deeper than her throat, though
she doubted very much that was why she felt so light-
headed.

But what she really noticed was her uncle's silence. He
didn't jump in to disabuse Atlas of his notion that Lexi
was an heiress to the Worth fortune. He didn't contradict
a single word Atlas had said.

He only sat there at the head of the table, looking colder
by the moment.

Which, as far as Lexi was concerned, might as well have been a billboard, screaming out the truth so it could be seen for miles in all directions.

"Do you really plan to marry him?" Uncle Richard asked her, after several eternities crawled by.

He didn't apologize for the past twenty years. He didn't explain why he'd let Lexi think she had nothing and more, was an often irritating charity case on top of that. He didn't justify his decision to make her live in a terrible flat and act like an everyday person when she had as much right to loaf around the estate collecting expensive things—not that she could imagine that kind of pointless life—as her cousins.

And when she'd walked in here tonight, Lexi'd had no intention of doing a single thing Atlas wanted. *Of course* she wasn't going to marry this man. This terrifying, brooding man bent on revenge who thought she owed him something. She had no intention of becoming his first casualty.

Especially when she thought—when she *knew*—that it would break what was left of her poor heart, the heart that had always been his, into a thousand pieces.

But Uncle Richard hadn't contradicted him. And that meant that her entire life was a deliberate, calculated fake. That her own family—her cousins and her uncle, the only relatives she had in the world—had perpetuated this lie all this time. They'd let her scrape and apologize and cater to them. They'd let her play the role of poor relation for years, hovering on the edge of their posh existence but never allowed any closer. They'd excluded her and condescended to her and acted as if she ought to be grateful for every scrap they'd grudgingly thrown her way.

What if Atlas hadn't come back? What if he'd never told her the truth? Would anyone at this table have done it for him?

For her?

That she already knew the answer made her feel something like dizzy.

She had no doubt that Atlas had planned that, too. That he'd planned all of this down to the smallest detail, including how betrayed she felt tonight. And there was a part of her that shrieked in warning at that.

There's no point jumping from the frying pan you know to the fire you don't, she tried to tell herself.

But she remembered what it had been like to be that lonely, terrified eight-year-old. Orphaned and alone. How grateful she'd been when her uncle had come to find her. How awed she'd been by Worth Manor when he'd brought her here.

And how he'd systematically broken her heart, one piece after the next, over the next twenty years. Excluding her here, making her feel unwelcome there. Reminding her she was little better than a servant one day, commanding her to hide herself away from view the next.

Bring on the fire, she thought then.

"Of course I'll marry Atlas," she heard herself say, with more bravado than certainty, and she even tipped her chin back in a show of defiance she wasn't entirely sure she wouldn't live to regret. "I can't wait."

CHAPTER FIVE

EVERYTHING WAS GOING according to plan.

Atlas had spent years refining the details of what he intended to do to the Worth family. Days turned into weeks, spread out into months. Year after year, he'd spun out scenarios and what-ifs and had carefully constructed what he believed to be the course of action not only most advantageous to him, but also most potentially upsetting for them.

And if anything, it was all even better than he'd hoped.

He would have used Lexi no matter what, of course. The moment his private investigators had uncovered the truth about her, and what Richard had been doing both to her and with her mother's fortune all these years, Atlas had understood that she was the key to everything he wanted. That he'd returned to England to discover that she was far more tempting and intriguing than he'd anticipated was merely icing on the whole, delicious cake of his post-prison life, he told himself.

But not if she was playing her own deep game.

Because what he hadn't expected was that it would be *so* easy. Almost too easy—to the point he began to worry that her sudden and complete acquiescence was a front. That she was stringing him along because it was easier and had no intention of truly bowing to his demands.

Which would not work. At all.

"Surely you should resist me a little, Lexi," he said several days after his return. "If only for show."

"I was unaware that resistance was permitted in this little game you're playing," Lexi replied, holding his gaze with that little hint of defiance that he found alternately compelling and concerning.

Because some part of him wondered if they were playing the same game—or two completely different ones. He didn't enjoy the sensation.

He'd sent a car to whisk her away from that lonely little carriage house out on the edge of Worth Manor grounds, where he knew they'd packed her away so they could keep pretending she wasn't the richest of the lot of them. Where they could make her feel like an afterthought. An imposition. He was an expert in the games the Worths played, having survived so many of them himself. The car delivered her directly to him in the showroom of one of his favorite couture houses in Mayfair. In the middle of the workday, whether she liked it or not.

But that was the thing. He couldn't quite tell if she liked it or didn't.

He couldn't quite read her, and Atlas had always prided himself on being able to read anyone. Everyone.

She was a funny little thing. Even now, she stood in the middle of what would have been paradise for another woman and looked…unmoved. Unaware, even, that she was standing in the midst of so much splendor. Gowns of every description hung here, there. Dressmakers' models covered in sumptuous fabrics dotted the floor. The women he'd known before jail would have been wreathed in delight, wandering back and forth and running their manicured fingers all over everything they could.

But that wasn't Lexi. Her hands were unmanicured. Her hair, unless he was very much mistaken and that was relatively rare, had not been cut by a stylist with any talent or vision in years. Maybe ever.

It was as if she *wanted* to be frumpy.

Atlas opted not to tell her that she was incapable of it, no matter what she thought she wanted. She was entirely too pretty to pretend otherwise—but that was the most startling thing about her. He didn't think she knew it.

Today she was wearing another one of her power suits, if that was what it could be called when the material involved was so shoddy. A dove-gray jacket and matching skirt that managed to completely conceal the shape of her body and the firm perfection of her curves. Atlas assumed that had to be a deliberate choice on her part. She'd marched in from the streets of fashionable, tony Mayfair as if she was risking life and limb in this notably high-class neighborhood, then stood there in the private room Atlas had requested as if facing a firing squad or two. She crossed her arms over her chest and scowled at him, though he would have said that the way she had her dark hair scraped back against her head should have prevented that much facial mobility.

"You can always attempt to resist, Lexi," Atlas murmured now, aware that he'd been staring at her—studying her—for entirely too long. Far past the point of anything resembling politeness. Then again, he was an ex-con. Politeness was no longer something he had to pretend was in his wheelhouse. "That doesn't mean you will be successful."

"Here's a funny little truth about me," Lexi said sweetly. The kind of sweetness that came with claws, and dug in. Deep. "I don't enjoy futility. I don't see the point of doing something if I know it's bound to fail."

"And what makes you think you're bound to fail?" Atlas asked mildly. "How terribly defeatist."

"I prefer to think of it as realistic, actually."

"Unless you win, of course. Is that realism or futility? I've lost track."

"I don't know what it is in a philosophical sense," she replied, a little shortly to his way of thinking, and she hadn't spent ten years in prison to earn her lack of civility. "What I do know is that it's unlikely. With you, anyway."

"That kind of attitude is a self-fulfilling prophecy, little one," he took a little too much joy in telling her. "I know. I never doubted I would escape my father's heavy hand, and so I did. I never doubted I would become a success far beyond the wildest imaginings of the drunk bastard who raised me, and I did exactly that, again and again. And I would not be sitting here today, a free man, if I had ever doubted there was any other outcome to my predicament."

Her brown eyes flashed with temper, and he watched her try to conceal that from him, fascinated against his will yet again. He'd expected this all to be entertaining, it was true, but once again he'd underestimated Lexi. He'd assumed that the amusement would come from the very fact that this was finally happening, that he was finally enacting the grand plans he'd spent so much time plotting out in his miserable cell. Or from the fact that he was at last restored to his former glory, perhaps. Or that he could lounge about in the showroom of one of England's most fashionable couture houses like some kind of pampered pasha and not worry that he might wake up at any moment to find himself back behind bars.

He'd spent a long time concocting the image of the perfect Worth bride to use for his purposes. He'd spent at least a whole year envisioning exactly what that would entail. The cut of her dress. The sinuous flow of her veil. And most important, the way she would appear on his arm and in all the photographs, like a princess defiled by the convict on her arm.

But there was something about Lexi that made him far less interested in the trappings and far more interested in her.

Atlas liked her. And he was trying very hard not to do such a foolish thing.

He couldn't have been more surprised. His memories of Lexi Haring were separated into two very discrete and separate parts. There was the pale, awkward shadow who had crept around behind Philippa, forever apologizing and cringing and shaking with embarrassment, except when he'd smiled at her. Then, she'd glowed; a girl with all the markings of the beautiful woman she would become, but no confidence whatsoever. He bore that poor child no particular ill will. He almost remembered her fondly, insofar as he had fond memories of any part of the life that had put him in jail.

But then there was the girl who'd sat up in that witness box, haltingly telling a story that he'd known—even as he sat there, listening to the prosecutor pull it out of her one damning word at a time—would be the end of him. He'd felt the jury turn against him with every word Lexi had gotten out, tears in her throat and trailing down her cheeks. He'd felt his freedom slip away, further and further out of his grasp with every second she'd sat there and condemned him.

To say he bore *that* version of Lexi some ill will would be understating his feelings on the subject. By a wide margin.

And still, neither memory had prepared him for the reality.

"I beg your pardon," she said stiffly now, having contained her initial flash of temper. Which he saw meant only that she stood taller. Tenser. "My distinct understanding of this whole plan of yours is that my failure is preordained. Isn't that the point of all of this?"

"It's not the point of it, no. A happy side effect, perhaps."

Her mouth twisted at that. "I'll refrain from beating my head against that wall, thank you."

"The beauty is in the struggle, little girl," Atlas said, low and possibly insulting, given the way she stiffened. "How else will you know you're alive?"

"I don't need to struggle to know I'm alive, Atlas," Lexi said, her brown eyes meeting his. Then holding.

He couldn't have said what it was he saw in them then. It wasn't anything so simple as defiance. He would have understood a rebellion. A fight. But instead, something in the way she looked at him made a most unpleasant sensation unwind, deep inside him, almost as if—

But no. Atlas didn't do shame. Ever.

"Why do you think you're here?" he asked her.

She eyed him for a minute, still standing there with her arms crossed, perhaps unaware that her body language broadcast the anxiety he assumed she'd have preferred to conceal. And he could have made this easier on her, he knew. He could have been friendly, for a start, or he could have stood up from the cozy little chair he lounged in like a lazy little king and done his best to put her at her ease.

Atlas didn't do any of those things.

He simply watched her, as if he was a member of the nobility from ages past and she was the woman he'd purchased to do his will. One way or another.

Because that was exactly what she was.

Whether she'd realized that yet or not.

He found himself more than a little intrigued that the diffident little shadow had grown up under Richard's oppressive thumb into…this. A woman who could have turned heads on the streets had she not gone to such lengths to conceal her beauty, wrapping it up in ugly suits and severe hairstyles.

"I find it better not to wonder petty things like *why* when receiving orders from the men who like to control my life," Lexi said after a moment, her voice calm. Though Atlas could see that far more hectic gleam in her gaze. He could tell she wasn't nearly as serene as she pretended.

He shook his head. "That's the saddest thing I have ever heard."

"What's the point of wasting my time like that?" Lexi asked, and there was an edge to her voice then. "My uncle did exactly as he pleased all this time with no one the wiser. I'm sure you will do the same. The only thing I can do is strap in and hope to survive it."

Atlas imagined she was trying to poke at him with that. What surprised him was that the blow landed. "You think your uncle Richard and I are similar?"

"Do you think you are not?" She looked around the showroom as if it spoke for itself. As if they were back in a courtroom and this time, she was taking on the role of prosecutor. "Manipulation is manipulation, Atlas. No matter your reasons."

"There are so many differences between me and your bastard of an uncle that I can hardly begin to name them," Atlas said, forcing himself to relax against the back of the chair despite the temper pounding through him. "But we'll try this one. I told you exactly what I was going to do. And why. Your uncle pulled you out of a flophouse when you were eight years old and told you that you were no better than a down market Cinderella. Nor did I hear him explain himself the other night when the truth about what he'd done to you was revealed. How is that similar?"

"You're right," Lexi retorted, her voice even but something bright and hot in her brown eyes. "You're a much better person. Plotting revenge for a decade and then racing here to carry it out is much, much better than lying by omission."

"Perhaps you're right and it's the same thing," Atlas mused. "You are ever the victim, Lexi. How does that feel?"

"Terrific. It feels absolutely *terrific*."

He didn't smile at that, though it was close. "Or perhaps the difference is that both you and I know exactly how complicit you are in what's happening to you now. You weren't an eight-year-old child, reeling from the loss of your parents ten years ago. You were eighteen. A legal adult. Wholly responsible for your own actions, I think we can agree."

"I was subpoenaed," Lexi bit out. "I had no choice but to testify."

"I do not recall subpoenaing you to marry me," Atlas drawled, propping up his head with one hand as if he was too lazy to remain upright. "Perhaps, if we are enjoying the spirit of all this honesty at last, it was what you wanted all along, no?"

He didn't actually think that was true, or he hadn't thought it. But the strangest thing happened when he said it. It was as if everything in him tensed in a kind of anticipation. As if he didn't just want to marry her because she was his permanent link to the Worth family and therefore the key to his revenge, but because he wanted to marry *her*. Lexi.

Atlas didn't know what to do with that.

Meanwhile, the effect of his words on Lexi was nothing short of electric. She jolted as if he'd plugged her directly into a wall socket, and even took a step back as if she needed to put more space between them. As if she needed the buffer.

Then Atlas watched as a bright red flush worked its way over her face, down her neck and splashed over what little of her chest he could see beneath that eyesore of a jacket she wore.

Atlas was no less affected. He felt the heat, wild and unmistakable, charge through him. His blood felt hot. His sex ached.

And not for *a woman*, as he wanted to tell himself.

For *this* woman, specifically, whether he liked it or not.

But he couldn't pursue the matter, because the door pushed open then and the lauded designer whose name was on the front of the building in huge gold letters swept in, all smiles.

"The happy couple!" she cried. "A thousand congratulations!"

And Atlas had to remind himself that what mattered here was not whether or not Lexi wanted to marry him. But that she would. That she felt she had no choice, because he had no intention of giving her one.

It was up to him to find a way to deal with the fact he found this woman more intriguing than he'd imagined he would. He sat back as the designer and her minions bustled around, flinging fabric this way and that. Taking measurements and draping things over Lexi where she stood. In his memories she was little more than a shadow and a wet face, and though he'd spent hours and hours in his cell imagining exactly what he would do to her, it was never *her* that he pictured. Not like this.

Not all grown up, with that mulish set to her jaw and a dark intelligence in her gaze. He'd certainly never imagined that she would grow up to possess that figure that he only began to appreciate in full as the dress designers encouraged her to disrobe. Behind a privacy screen, of course—but then she was standing before him on the little stand in the center of the room rid at last of her ill-fitting power suit and wearing nothing at all but bolts of fabric draped this way and that.

His mouth went dry.

Atlas tried to tell himself it was a function of the decade of celibacy that had been forced upon him, that he would have found any half-naked female precisely this compelling, but he wasn't sure he believed his own excuses.

Because everyone else in the room was female, too, yet the only woman he could seem to focus on at all was Lexi.

She looked different when he could see the beguiling line of her clavicle and the gentle slope of her arms, all cream and satin. She looked softer with all her silky brown hair let loose to swirl around her shoulders. Younger and sweeter, and something a good deal more like vulnerable when she met his eyes in the mirror.

"You see?" the head designer asked, smiling. "She will be the most beautiful bride who ever walked down an aisle."

"I have no doubt," he agreed. "I am a lucky man, is that not so, Lexi *mou*?"

The Greek endearment came a little too easily, but it was worth it. In the mirror, he saw a stricken expression move across Lexi's face as she nodded—but only, he knew, because others were watching. He saw that sheen of shame and worry and something more painful still in her gaze and the way she quickly lowered her eyes. And he was enough of a monster to enjoy it.

Oh, yes, Atlas thought with intense satisfaction as the designers crafted the dress he wanted, right there in front of him. And the bride to go with it, who would make all his vengeful dreams come true.

This was going far better than he ever could have imagined.

The papers, of course, were beside themselves.

Every day the paparazzi gathered in a thick little scrum outside the front door of the house in Belgravia that had stood empty this past decade awaiting Atlas's return, horrifying his neighbors around the garden square. They shouted the same questions at him, over and over, every time he made an appearance. And they delighted in the answers he gave, because everyone loved a story like Atlas's.

They'd loved it when he'd clawed his way out of the Greek gutters. They'd loved it when he'd scaled the heights of the corporate world. They'd adored it when he'd fallen. And they were obsessed with him even more now that he was back, with a complicated tale of betrayal and suffering ready-made for the kind of dramatic fictions that were the tabloids' stock in trade.

He'd waited so long for this. To have microphones in his face again, and not because he was a once powerful man being carted off into prison. He was accordingly expansive. Detailed. Calling out the Worth family in as many ways as he could, every day, without actually naming them directly.

"A man can tolerate a great many things," he said gravely one morning on his way to work, as if it had only just occurred to him. "But it is always the casual betrayal of those he believes to be friends that keeps him up at night."

Atlas Puts Worths on Blast! the papers screamed.

"Is it entirely necessary for you to prosecute a private family matter in those ratty tabloids you love so much?" Richard asked the following morning.

He'd come to find Atlas in the offices that Atlas had reclaimed at the Worth Trust headquarters. Atlas had been deep into a series of calls to crucial business associates, rounding up their support and pledges of loyalty now that he was the most infamous CEO alive. He'd looked up from a pile of supplementary papers the secretarial staff had provided him to see Richard standing there, looking faintly ill at ease in the doorway to the office. Not that Atlas trusted that. Not when it came to Richard Worth, who had made a cottage industry out of feeling entirely comfortable with whatever he did.

As with everything in this place of lies and betrayals, he had to assume it was an act. Because it was all an act. Always. He would never forgive himself for failing to see that the first time around.

"I was unaware that I was prosecuting anything at all," Atlas replied. He stood there behind his old desk, the one he'd chosen himself all those years ago when he'd gotten the position and had thought he'd finally made it. When after all the struggle and determination, he'd finally arrived. He'd been sure of it. "I can only tell my story, Richard. I apologize if it's not a tale that pleases you."

"I think we both know that you have no interest whatsoever in pleasing me. Quite the contrary."

Atlas inclined his head. "I cannot say it is a goal of mine, no. But I'm not necessarily opposed to it, either."

"What is it you want?" Richard asked.

The way he kept asking, as if he thought that if he repeated the question enough times and in enough ways, it would elicit a different answer.

Atlas only smiled. "These are the happiest days of my life, Richard," he said quietly. With a dark menace he made no attempt to hide. "I am a free man and soon to be a married one. Has a man alive ever known such joy? I think not."

Richard's lips thinned with obvious displeasure. "You might be able to manipulate that poor girl—"

Atlas laughed. "I think you'll find *that poor girl* is not only grown, but not as easily bent to your will as you imagine. You probably shouldn't have lied to her for all these years."

He wondered if Richard would take this opportunity— alone, with no one to overhear him, and without Lexi right there in front of him to react to whatever it was he might say—to come clean about his motivations. Or to admit what he'd done all these years because there had been no one to call him on it. No one who knew the truth about Yvonne's fortune.

But he should have known better. This was Richard Worth. He admitted nothing—likely because he imagined he couldn't do anything wrong. If he did something—any-thing—it was by definition right and correct. Atlas was familiar with the way the old man thought.

"Where do you think this will end?" Richard asked instead, shaking his head as if this all made him deeply sad. Which was laughable. "What do you think is going to happen here?"

"Don't you worry, Richard," Atlas said, still smiling. "You won't be in any doubt about my intentions. I prom-ise you."

And so it was that a scant few weeks after he'd been exonerated and released from prison, Atlas stood up in the famous little chapel on the rolling green lawn at Worth Manor in a morning suit especially crafted to make him look as lethal as he did elegant, and waited for the last re-maining Worth heiress to walk down the aisle and make him her husband.

In a way, he'd been waiting for this his whole life. With or without the little decade-long plot twist of that Massachusetts prison. In some ways, he could hardly reconcile himself to the man he'd been back then. The brash, arrogant young man who'd assumed that his position with the Worth family was the beginning of a great, golden age that would never end. That would shine on and on, making him bigger and brighter and better than even he had been able to imagine.

But even then, he'd wanted it to lead here. Right here. Standing in the family chapel, cementing himself as forever a part of them. Complete with eventual children that linked him by blood to these people.

Whether they wanted it or not.

He let his gaze sweep over the assembled congregation. The pews were packed tight with the inevitable *Who's Who* of fashionable London crammed in next to corporate London, and half of Europe besides. The full-throated supporters who had stood by him during his incarceration pressed against those who had thrown him under any and all available buses, and with gusto.

He wanted to rub this in the faces of that latter group.

In the front row sat the tedious Gerard and his painfully self-satisfied wife, flanked by their three plain-faced, sullen children. Harry sat beside them, looking like some kind of red-faced, furious carrot while his brother and sister-in-law did their best to maintain what passed for their stoic expressions.

Atlas smiled warmly at them for the simple, petty joy of watching them all glare back at him.

But then the music started and he dismissed them.

Because it was finally happening. In the next hour he would secure himself the precise future he'd dreamed of while stuck in that cell. He would insert himself into this family that had exalted and vilified him. He would claim it as his own.

At last.

The doors at the back of the chapel opened and Richard stepped through them, Lexi on his arm.

"I will walk myself down the aisle," Lexi had told him fiercely when Atlas had told her how he envisioned the ceremony.

She'd appeared to be laboring under the misconception that he'd been soliciting her opinions and input.

"That will not work for me," he had told her. Mildly enough, he'd thought, when he'd been astonished that she'd dared contradict him.

"I don't see why not. It's my wedding, too." She'd been sitting stiffly in the seat opposite him in the restaurant he'd chosen for its large glass windows, the better for their "romance" to be seen and discussed breathlessly in all the papers. "Though you don't seem particularly interested in that fact."

"Of course it is your wedding, too," Atlas had replied smoothly, signaling the waiter who hovered nearby for more wine. "And I want you to enjoy it. I do. Provided you do exactly as I say, Lexi, I'm sure we will both enjoy ourselves tremendously."

And as the waiter had dutifully refilled their glasses, Atlas had wondered if she would defy him. Here in this restaurant or perhaps later, when there were cameras aimed at her. He'd realized over the course of their warp-speed engagement that he couldn't predict what she might do at any moment. Lexi seemed so meek, so scared of her own shadow, most of the time. And then every now and again there would be that flash of spirit in her gaze and there was no telling what she might do next.

If he was honest, he liked that more than he should.

But still, in the matter of Richard escorting her down the aisle, at least, he was pleased to discover she'd obeyed him.

Maybe more pleased than he should have been, as if the obedience of his cowed and conquered enemy was some kind of gift.

The dress was exactly as he'd pictured it, a fairy-tale confection of a wedding gown that befit a wealthy heiress marrying a very rich and powerful man. As if his bride was her own cake, a sweet explosion of white lace and full, flowing skirts. It was perfect. He could already see the way the dress itself would claim the real estate on the front page of every possible paper. The ones he'd already made deals with and the ones who would simply poach the exclusive photographs. She looked like a fairy princess, and he would look like the devil beside her, a dark and grim threat of an ex-con, and it was all precisely the way he'd wanted it.

But what he hadn't anticipated was *her*. Lexi herself.

She had surprised him repeatedly in the quick run-up to the wedding, but he still hadn't been prepared. Not for this. Not for her.

Because the fact was, she was more than simply beautiful. Something about her got to him, as if she was wedged beneath his skin. He thought of her too often. He was afraid he'd even dreamed of her. She was slowly driving him mad.

And Atlas understood that he was in terrible trouble.

Because all the planning, all the plotting, all the teasing out of this or that outcome in his head, had not prepared him for the simple reality of standing in that ancient chapel, with the wedding march playing and the eyes of the world upon him, watching her walk toward him.

He had considered the wedding a necessary part of his plan, but a means to an end, really. A necessary spectacle en route to his total and complete power grab of everything the Worths held dear, and better still, a symbol of the way they would hand it all to him.

Whatever he wanted. Whatever he asked

Because it was the very least they owed him.

But in all that plotting, he'd somehow managed to avoid thinking too closely about his bride. He just assumed that he could make over any pale shadow into an appropriate princess for the day, because that was the easy part. A few sessions with a stylist and a good fitting and *boom*, anyone could look the part.

Even awkward, deceitful little Lexi.

What he hadn't anticipated was…this.

The constriction in his chest. The roaring in his ears. The intense need like a fist, gripping his sex. His chest. *Him*.

Lexi Haring had been hiding her light all this time, just as he'd suspected. That was the first thing Atlas noticed, because today, she shone. She fairly *beamed*.

Today she wore her hair swept back and up, but not in one of the headache-inducing buns she preferred. It was much softer today, curls tumbling here and there behind her, the front part held up with the same gleaming clip that held her veil in place. He could see her face beneath the sheer fabric, her full lips, fine little nose and those depthless brown eyes that seemed to slam into him from down at the other end of the aisle.

In his fantasies, he'd expected to lord it over Richard as the old man walked half of his net worth down the aisle to hand her over into Atlas's greedy, upstart hands, and he felt that as a kind of triumph. That victory.

But he couldn't seem to look away from Lexi.

It was as if nothing existed save the two of them.

He didn't know what the hell was happening to him.

Atlas was distantly aware of the vicar behind him. The crowd before him. But it was Lexi who commanded the whole of his attention as she and her uncle came to a stop before him. Lexi who seemed to blot out the rest of the world, simply by standing there, looking up at him.

Almost as if—

But he didn't believe in that, either.

The vicar said something, and Richard transferred Lexi's hand from his arm to Atlas's grip. And that should have been a powerful moment. A sweet kick of revenge. Atlas knew that, somewhere inside him. He saw the look of distaste that Richard didn't try very hard to hide. He knew that this moment ate at the older man, just as he'd anticipated.

But he couldn't seem to focus on his revenge. Not when Lexi's delicate little fingers were curled over his. Not when it was time to push back her veil and let the full force of her pretty face and that wary innocence in her dark eyes slam into him like a blow.

He hadn't been expecting this. He hadn't expected her to be anything but a means to an end.

And yet there was nothing to do, then—stood up in front of the world on an altar with so many of his enemies looking on—but surrender to it.

Atlas told himself no one would know.

He stood up at the front of that church, he said the necessary words and no one but him would ever be the wiser. No one but him would ever know that for longer than he cared to contemplate, the only thing he was aware of in all the world was the woman who stood at his side, resplendent in the dress he'd had made just for her.

No one would know that for the whole of the wedding ceremony, the only thing he thought about was Lexi. And him. Together.

And not what their marriage would do for him, but what she might permit him to do to her.

No one could see inside his head. No one could see the

images that tortured him, one after the next, each more decadent and tempting than the last.

Atlas had been without a woman for a long, long time. And he hadn't married Lexi for sex. Or anyway, that hadn't been the motivating factor.

But as he took her hand and slid on the wedding ring he'd chosen specifically because it was heavy—much like a shackle, or like the handcuffs her words had put him in years ago—it occurred to him that he was going to enjoy married life a great deal more than he'd anticipated.

Something he confirmed when he brushed her mouth with his to claim his wife at last, barely a kiss at all, and he could still feel it everywhere. Like a burst of flame, searing him where he stood. And he knew, then.

He was going to have to rethink the cold, quiet, distant marriage of pure convenience he'd imagined, because Atlas had every intention of eating Lexi alive.

Again and again and again.

He could hardly wait to get started.

CHAPTER SIX

LEXI HAD NEVER spent a lot of time imagining her wedding.

There had never seemed to be any particular point to it. Philippa had been the one with grand daydreams about princess gowns in glorious ballrooms on the arm of Prince Charmings who changed by the week. Lexi had always imagined that if it ever happened for her, it would be a much more modest affair. A trip to the register office, no muss and no fuss. Perhaps a small meal down at the local pub. Nothing fancy, because she had never imagined herself to be anything but the poor little relation Uncle Richard had always told her she was, lucky to have a job and a flat.

She'd never wanted more than that. Or at least, she hadn't thought she'd wanted more.

And she was therefore astonished at how easy it was to lose herself in the fantasy of this wedding that Atlas had thrown. She hadn't been able to sleep for days now, tossing and turning the nights away, because she'd been so certain that she was going to feel like some kind of alien in the bridal gown Atlas insisted she wear. She was convinced not only that she was being forced to play an ill-fitting role, but also that everyone would stare at her while she did it, entirely too aware of what a reach it was.

But the strangest thing happened when she slipped into the deceptively comfortable dress. She liked it.

She might not have recognized herself, exactly, but Lexi liked how she felt in all that whisper-soft fabric, made up to look like exactly the sort of woman she'd never imagined she'd be.

Pretty, for a start.

She'd waited in a small room at the back of the chapel in her marvelous dress, alone, sneaking little glances at the reflection she hardly recognized in the mirror. She'd listened to the sounds of all the people entering and had wondered if she ought to feel nervous. Agitated. But something about climbing into the dress had soothed her. It wasn't until Uncle Richard had stormed into the antechamber and taken her arm that she'd felt as if she was moments away from breaking out into some kind of prickly heat at the contact.

"You don't have to do this," he had said.

It had sounded a good deal more like a suggestion than support.

Lexi had stared up at this man whom she'd once imagined was her savior. At that long, saturnine face of his that she decided years ago was kind.

Based on absolutely no evidence.

"And what then?" she'd asked him, impressed with herself when she sounded so calm. So cool. "What do you imagine will become of any of us if Atlas doesn't get what he wants?"

"Is this what he wants?" Her uncle had eyed her as if he'd always harbored suspicions about the kind of person she was. Maybe he had. "Or what you want?"

"What *I* want?" she'd echoed. She'd almost burst out into laughter, she'd been so stunned. "I beg your pardon. When has what *I* want mattered to another living soul?"

Her uncle had only stared at her.

"Is that what you told my mother?" she heard herself ask him.

Uncle Richard's face had turned to stone. "I told her what would happen if she disobeyed me. Unfortunately, Lexi, your mother was little more than a whore."

Lexi hadn't broken out in a rash. She hadn't quailed. She hadn't even averted her eyes. All those years of practice had come in handy.

And her voice had been perfectly even when she'd replied. "But not, it turns out, a penniless one."

Soon enough, the music had started, the doors had been thrown open and her stone-cold, frozen uncle had led her down that aisle. All of them dancing to Atlas's tune in one way or another. All of them paying for the sins of the past.

All of them pawns in Atlas's game.

Lexi had taken her courage from the dress and the way it danced around her as she moved. She'd taken solace from the fact that like it or not, this was likely the only wedding she would ever have—and certainly the fanciest, because the fortune she still couldn't quite believe was hers was obviously something Atlas viewed as his own, personal compensation—and that meant she could give herself leave to enjoy it. If she could.

However she could.

And then she'd seen Atlas.

His gaze had slammed into her from the end of the chapel aisle, hard and proud, black and commanding, and it was as if her body was no longer hers. As if *she* was no longer her own. As if he could reach down the length of the chapel aisle with only that gaze of his and take control of her that easily.

And the craziest part was, it felt natural. *Right.*

It felt like heat and light and something else she was

afraid to name, because it felt a good deal worse than a simple *crush*.

And Lexi didn't need anyone to tell her how dangerous that was. How remarkably, mind-numbingly foolish. She knew. Of course she knew.

But now it was worse. Much worse.

Now she was his wife.

The wedding breakfast had plodded along, taking over the whole of the formal dining hall at Worth Manor. There was dancing in the ballroom, and the grounds had been manicured and plumped to within an inch of their lives. The morning's early rain had given way to a tremulous blue sky, and Lexi tried her best to keep from thinking unhelpful and deeply silly things.

Like the blue was a kind of harbinger of hope and peace, and all of this would end well.

Because she knew better. This wasn't the beginning of anything. This was the end that Atlas had planned a long time ago. And she might have felt like a princess in the glorious gown that swished when she walked and felt like a caress against her legs and thighs, but she wasn't.

She'd hardly had any time to digest the fact that she wasn't the poor, lowly relation she'd always considered herself—and now it didn't matter. Because Atlas had claimed her and one thing she knew for certain was that he would do what he wished.

Exactly what he wished, with as little consideration for her feelings on the matter as possible.

Which she thought might be a good thing, because her feelings were…problematic.

They were the same as they'd ever been, only now Lexi wondered if this was the silly crush she'd thought it was all those years ago. Or if it was instead something far more dangerous.

The reception sprawled over all the public rooms of the great house. Flowers bloomed in sleek arrangements on every surface, and the house seemed lighter, brighter, than it had in years. And Lexi smiled as she spoke to all the people who'd demanded she run and fetch them cups of tea a few weeks back, yet now treated her with excruciating deference.

If she didn't think about it too closely, it was even fun.

"You don't have to obey him," Harry told her as the reception wore on. He was drunk, as usual. Or that was what Lexi assumed, given the bright shade of red in his nose and cheeks. She wished she hadn't dutifully gone to him when he'd peremptorily signaled her from his position against one wall in one of the salons. "This isn't the bloody Dark Ages."

She tried to afford him the same smile she'd given everyone today, but thought she fell a little short. Not that he noticed. "I don't know what that means."

"It means that you're a modern girl, Lexi," Harry said, but there was that flat look in his eyes. And that curl to his lips. And Lexi didn't really like how close he was standing, but thought it would be far more trouble than it was worth to either step back or tell him to give her some space. She made do with gritting her teeth. "You can do as you like. Surely you know that. Wedding or no wedding, you can decide to do whatever you want."

"Imagine my surprise to discover your feminist side, Harry," Lexi said drily, when she was sure she could speak without rolling her eyes. "I wouldn't have pegged you for pink hat and a long march as an ally of the cause."

"Don't be ridiculous." Harry tossed back more of his drink. He wasn't even looking at her. Lexi followed his dark glare and found he was aiming it at Atlas, across the room neck deep in a pack of European businessmen. "All I'm saying is, good on you for giving him what he wanted. But that doesn't mean you need to give him everything he wants, if you know what I mean."

"I don't," she said. "I don't have the slightest idea what you mean."

She'd only said that to be obstinate, but the way Harry looked at her then made her skin crawl.

"Then I guess you're nothing but his whore," Harry said, in a deceptively friendly tone that made it worse. Much, much worse. "And bad things happen to whores, Lexi. You might want to remember that."

And he'd left her there, suddenly cold, as he lurched off to find a new drink to drown himself in.

Lexi kept her smile plastered to her face, because she didn't dare let it drop. She had no idea what her expression might show. And she didn't want to let herself think about the fact that two separate members of the Worth family had thrown the word *whore* in her face today.

Uncle Richard had obviously acted on it with Lexi's mother. He'd thrown Yvonne off the property and had told her she was disowned. Was that the sort of threat Harry had been leveling at her?

Or had he been hinting at something much darker? Lexi thought back to that summer, and the trouble Philippa had found it so amusing to get into with the American boys she met on those white sand Martha's Vineyard beaches. Had Harry thought Philippa was a whore, too?

Did all the Worth "whores" end up dead?

Lexi felt cold. And then she felt her neck prickle and looked up to find Atlas regarding her in his usual dark way from where he stood with a different passel of jolly corporate types.

The trouble was, he was the biggest threat of all and yet she didn't feel threatened when he looked at her. Or at least, not in the way she did when Harry spoke to her in that tone or her uncle looked at her as if she was a worm.

But Atlas simply took her breath away.

There was no pretending otherwise today. Something had happened during the ceremony. Or maybe she didn't have enough experience to tell either way, but she didn't think she needed experience to tell that there had been something in the way Atlas held her hand on that altar. There had been something in the expression on his hard, cruel face as he'd gazed down at her.

Something more than the blaze of dark triumph in his eyes. Something more complicated than the simple victory of a man bent on revenge.

She was sure of it.

But that didn't help her now. Or when, some time and many forcedly cheerful conversations with strangers later, Atlas finally came to collect her.

"Are you ready, wife?" he asked.

That word, *wife*, made her shiver. And not the way Harry had.

Atlas had kept his distance throughout the breakfast and the reception. Lexi couldn't tell if it was deliberate or not. On the one hand, she thought Atlas considered everything he did, in minute detail and far in advance. But on the other, she knew that he had far greater aspirations than whatever it was he planned to do to her. So it hadn't completely surprised her that he'd spent their wedding circulating amongst the guests. Reintroducing himself to those who might have written him off while he'd been in prison, and effortlessly reminding everyone in the room that he was Atlas Chariton, back and at full power. Not to mention entirely too charming when he put his mind to it, magnetic and impossible to ignore.

Not, of course, that she'd tried all that hard to ignore him.

"Ready?" she echoed.

"Surely you haven't forgotten already," he murmured, that dark amusement flitting over his face as he took her hand. And she hoped she managed to cover the lick of flame that moved through her at that contact, making her think he might burn her down where she stood. "You married me this very day. Now, I'm afraid, the time has come to leave the adoring crowd and come play wife to your new husband."

"I…" She was afraid she would stutter the way she hadn't in years, so she stopped. She swallowed, and thought he could actually hear her when she did it. "Where are we going? You never really talked about anything past the wedding ceremony."

"Surely you know what comes next." Atlas's smile was far darker then, and far more dangerous. "Some think it's the best part."

"Are you…" She wanted to slap herself. Her heart was beating too fast, her stomach was in knots and she couldn't seem to form the words she needed. As if her mouth was mounting its own kind of resistance—except it felt a good deal like weakness. "You can't possibly be talking about sex."

That smile of his moved over his mouth, sardonic and hard and entirely too beguiling. "Can I not?"

"Oh. Well. We've never talked about that."

He did something with her hand, though she couldn't have said what. One moment his fingers were around hers, which was confronting enough, and then the next it was as if he'd lit her on fire. Then he tugged, and she was so off balance that she thought she might have crumpled to the floor had he not caught her up against his wide, broad chest.

"What is there to talk about?"

Atlas leaned down as if he wanted to tell her a secret. Or maybe it just felt that way, because when he was that close it was as if nothing existed but the two of them. Not the reception all around them, teeming with so many watchful eyes. Not anything.

"Everything, I'd think," she managed to say, though she wasn't sure her words made a sound.

She felt more than heard the laughter that moved through him then, dark and intense, and somehow ended up inside her, too.

"I like sex, Lexi," he told her, setting off a thousand more fires inside her. "I more than like it. And I have every intention of having rather a lot of it with the woman I married. Unless you have some objection?"

She fought off another debilitating shiver that seemed to start so low in her belly it was almost between her legs, and then she put a little space between them. Just a little, so she could look up at him, past the acres of his steel-hewn chest in the morning suit that made him look almost good enough to eat. She realized she'd braced her hands against him and had the distant thought that she really shouldn't be touching him. But she didn't stop.

"You don't want me," she said, more severely than she'd intended, frowning up at him. "You don't have to pretend. Just to…" She shrugged, the movement of her shoulders feeling sharp. Something like angry, though she didn't think she was. She felt too many things, all of them textured and weighted and messy. *Angry* was simplest. "I've already married you. You don't have to play these games."

She expected his ire, but instead he looked…curious. And something else she couldn't quite put her finger on. Almost fascinated, except that didn't make sense. This was Atlas Chariton. He had far bigger fish to fry than Lexi.

"What game do you think I'm playing?" he asked, and she got the distinct impression he was amused again. Or still.

"The sex stuff," she said dismissively. As if she could wave her hand and stop caring about this. *Or about him*, something in her whispered. "I agreed to this marriage, but I already know it's one of convenience, nothing more. It doesn't need to be anything but that."

"Ah, but it does." Atlas held her when she pushed against him, not allowing her to gain even a sliver more space between their bodies. And what was wrong with her that she liked his offhanded show of strength? That rather than make her feel trapped, it made her feel something perilously close to safe? "It needs to be a great deal more than that, as a matter of fact. Didn't I mention this?"

"What you want is the fortune I didn't even know I had, and the opportunity to rub it in my uncle's face." Lexi worked hard to keep her expression neutral because it was suddenly important to her—crucially important, though she couldn't have said why—that she seem as unbothered and unfazed by this conversation as possible. "You've already accomplished that."

Atlas reached over with his free hand and tugged on one of those long, loose curls that made Lexi feel far more feminine than she could remember feeling in years. That was dangerous, because the more feminine she felt around Atlas, the more her body urged her to do the kinds of things she suspected might destroy her. Like lean a little closer. Or stand in that way she knew other women did, particularly around him, sticking out their chests and batting their eyelashes. That wasn't her. She had never had the urge to do any of those things in her life.

But everything today was different.

She was different.

"I thought you understood, Lexi *mou*," Atlas said quietly, something infinitely dangerous in his dark eyes. "This is a long game."

"It's your game. Not mine."

"My game, your game, it doesn't matter. It's going to require a little bit more from you than standing around looking decorative in a white dress, I'm afraid."

He sounded almost apologetic when she knew he wasn't. Of course he wasn't.

"I only do what I'm told," Lexi told him. She didn't know where those words came from. Much less the way she threw them at him, like bullets. "That's my role, isn't it? My uncle, you. I just follow orders. My understanding is that makes me a whore."

If she expected that to shame him, she was in for a surprise. Atlas only smiled—a dark, decidedly male curve of his mouth. "Then our wedding night will be even better than I'd imagined."

"So this really is about sex." She thought she sounded brave. Or she tried, anyway. "Why not simply say so?"

"This is about a great many things," Atlas told her, and that smile changed. It grew sharp edges and seemed to wedge itself deep into her gut. "But as far as you're concerned? It's all about the sex. Because I plan to use your body in every possible way, Lexi. I've been saving up. I have years and years of aggression to work out, all over your sweet, little bottom."

She was dimly aware that someone was breathing too hard. And it took her long moments to understand that it was her.

"This was never going to be decorous." Atlas showed no signs of altered breathing. His black gaze was hot. Hard. It was everything and it was shattering her where she stood—yet she couldn't seem to make herself move away. "This was never going to be easy. I plan to own every square inch of your skin."

She tried to say something then, but only his name came out, as soft as a whisper. Rather more plea than complaint, she was all too aware.

"Is that better?" Atlas asked. "Do you feel more prepared?"

"I assume that's the last thing you want." Her voice was barely a whisper. Lexi understood that probably gave her away—let him see how vulnerable she felt, how scared and overwhelmed and whatever that other, giddier thing was that felt almost too sharp to bear—but she couldn't worry about that then. "If I feel prepared, you can't possibly cause as much damage as you plan. And then what will you do?"

She didn't know what she expected, but it wasn't the strange, simmering way that Atlas looked down at her then. It wasn't that odd shadow in his too-black gaze. Or the way his hand moved from tugging on the end of that curl to brush briefly over her cheek.

So briefly she almost thought she'd imagined it, had her heart not tripped over itself at his touch.

"You can call it damage if you want," Atlas said quietly. "I won't contradict you. But I think you and I both know that the only thing I'm really going to damage here is your pride. And you can survive that, believe me. You might not enjoy it. You might hate what you find on the other side of the things you cling to and wish were real. But you will survive it all the same."

He didn't explain that, but then, Lexi was terrified that

there was a part of her that didn't require any explanation. Because her brain might have revolted at that, but her body had quite a different reaction. As if it knew things she didn't.

And the worst part was, she suspected that Atlas knew all those same things, too.

He swept her from the hall and Lexi went along with him by rote. Because she couldn't think of what else to do and worse—she couldn't quite muster up the necessary energy to defy him. It was almost as if she didn't *want* to defy him.

She waved. She smiled. She let him usher her into the restored old classic car that waited for them, and she sat there in a mute sort of acceptance as they swept out the long Worth Manor drive and into the London streets.

Do something, she ordered herself, but it was as if she was trapped inside a kind of prison inside her own body, unable to do a thing.

And the truth was, what could she do? She had no safe spaces left. Once Atlas had announced their engagement, she'd been swarmed by paparazzi every time she set foot off the Worth Manor grounds. Her flat had been inaccessible—and it wasn't as if she'd ever found the sad old bedsit to be much of a retreat.

Still, she hadn't liked it when Atlas had informed her she couldn't go back there.

"You should thank me for making certain you can't return to that revolting place," he'd told her on one of their "dates," which had involved a great many proclamations like that one, delivered in public places where she could only nod and smile in return, to the tune of a hundred flashbulbs.

"*That revolting place* is my home."

"I've floated a story to explain it," Atlas had informed

her, running right over her like the runaway train he was. "We cannot allow anyone to suspect that your dear uncle had no intention of ever handing over your fortune to you, of course."

That wasn't something she wanted to think about. She was afraid of what would happen once she did. "You can't possibly want to protect him."

"Not at all." Atlas had smiled in that way he did, that had made goose bumps shiver up and down her arms. "But I prefer to keep that in reserve. For better use later on."

"I don't see what that has to do with my flat."

"The public will not accept an heiress in a hovel." He'd shrugged when she glared at him. "Therefore, I've let it be known in a few key corners that you were so appalled by what happened to Philippa that you vowed you'd live a modest, humble life instead."

"Why would anyone believe that? It's ridiculous."

"The eccentric rich are a British pastime," Atlas had replied with another shrug that reminded her how very Greek he was. "Besides, it's so delightfully poetic, is it not? Our great love was torn apart a decade ago and there we both sat and suffered in our respective prisons, hardly daring to hope we might be reunited again."

Lexi had sniffed. "You ought to write for Mills and Boon."

"My understanding is that romance novels come with a happy ending," Atlas had replied smoothly. Horribly. "This, Lexi, is life. Not a romance novel. You have no such guarantee."

But it hadn't mattered what she'd said. Her uncle had informed her the next day that he was having her things—such as they were—packed up and she was to remain on the estate, in one of the bedchambers in the carriage house.

Bedchambers that had been there as long as she'd

worked at Worth Manor, yet had somehow never been offered to her before. Not that she was counting all the ways her uncle had treated her badly.

Because she couldn't count that high and anyway, there was no point going down that road. Lexi understood it was a one-way trip.

She sat where she was in the back of the restored old car, hands folded in her lap and her spine as straight as it would go without actually hurting herself, gazing out the window as the city slipped past. Next to her, Atlas made no attempt to touch her—which made her more certain with every second that he could do so at any moment. Her pulse drummed at her, anticipating what he might do every time he breathed, but he didn't do a thing.

Instead, he pulled out his phone and made calls. In Greek, in case she might have imagined she could take the opportunity of all this odd intimacy to eavesdrop.

Atlas, she noticed, seemed perfectly at his ease.

Of course he does, she snapped at herself. *He's in complete control of everything that's happened since they let him out of that prison cell.*

Unlike Lexi, who hadn't been in control of a blessed thing in as long as she could remember. Maybe longer.

When they arrived at the Belgravia town house Lexi remembered Atlas purchasing outright years ago, to the endless delight of the press and the quietly tutted consternation of her uncle and his fat-cat friends, Atlas ushered her out of the car as if he'd done so a thousand times before. His hand fit entirely too easily in the small of her back. Worse, he reached for her with a certain masculine ease that made her feel too hot, everywhere.

And when he stood next to her outside the home that had marked him all those years ago as a powerful force to be reckoned with—and perhaps, now that she considered it, as a target—she had the strangest notion that she'd been crafted just for him.

It was the way she fit right there beside him. As if, had they been different people, she could have rested her head against one of his wide, sculpted shoulders. Or tipped herself forward, tilted her head back and lost herself in a kiss.

She was appalled at the very thought, of course. Or so she told herself, sternly, as he led her inside.

Into his lair, that voice inside her intoned, because the voice inside her was deeply unhelpful.

She didn't know what she expected from his house, but it wasn't what she found when she stepped inside. From the outside, the Belgravia house was like any other on the stately old garden square, teeming with greenery and trees that were locked away for the enjoyment of the residents, not the grubby public. It was gleaming white, as befit the neighborhood and the period in which it had been built.

But inside, the house had been gutted and modernized. It was now an eclectic mix of contemporary spaces and clever period details, tossed together so it felt something like new. Different. Masculine grays and steel accents. Bold, uncompromising art.

Quintessentially Atlas, she would have said. Unexpected, just as he was, and yet perfect all the same.

Though she would never have said such a thing *to* him.

"Welcome to your new home," he said from beside her, and she had to control the urge to jump a foot or two in the air at his voice *so close* to her. Dark and low, rolling through her like a coming storm.

"Home?" she asked. Something about that word made her skin feel too tight over her bones.

"Yes, Lexi." He sounded lazy, and yet with a hint of patience sorely tried. "Surely you cannot imagine any scenario in which my wife will continue to live separately, in a carriage house on another man's property, can you?"

"I can't say I really thought about it."

He shook his head at her. "We've been married less than half a day and you're already lying to me. This hardly sets a decent precedent, does it?"

She pressed her lips together and waited for the racket inside her chest to subside.

"Fine," she said coolly. "The truth is that it never occurred to me that there was anything the slightest bit real about this marriage. I was under the impression I'm nothing to you but the human equivalent of a safety deposit box. Obviously, I didn't imagine that included shared living spaces."

Atlas studied her, his dark eyes gleaming. "Your imagination is sorely lacking, but do not let that worry you, Lexi. Mine is nothing if not vivid."

She swallowed at that, but looked away from him, at the house. It was huge, like all the houses in the area. A morning room bled into a study and she thought she saw a library down a stately hall.

"I suppose I can move from a West London bedsit to a sprawling Belgravia mansion," she murmured. "Though that seems like a downgrade, obviously."

If he found that amusing, he didn't show it.

"To clarify, little one, you will live here, in my house. With me. That means in my bed, not safely tucked away in a guest room behind a bolted door, or off in a separate wing where you will never see me." His dark brows rose when she stared at him with a shock she couldn't conceal. "That is what a wife does, after all. Surely you are aware of this."

"I'm surprised at how domestic you are." If asked, she would have sworn that she didn't mean to be provoking, but clearly her mouth had other ideas. And anyway, he didn't ask. "It's not necessarily a bad thing. Though I'm not convinced it goes with your whole *give me revenge or give me death* persona."

She should have known better than to imagine that would get to him. His smile was lazy, as always. If there was any edginess, it was in her. Scraping her hollow from the inside out as she stood there in her pretty gown and tried to pretend she was unaffected.

"Oh, little girl." His voice was so soft. All threat and darkness, and yet it throbbed in her like heat. "You have no idea. Revenge isn't a one-size-fits-all proposition. But don't worry. You'll learn."

Her throat was suddenly dry, but Atlas moved that too-penetrating gaze from her and that was marginally better. He strode deeper into the house and she followed him, because he'd tilted his head in a wordless command and he'd bought her, hadn't he? Or bargained for her, anyway.

That was the reason she clung to then, as if it would explain her behavior.

She glanced around as she followed him, taking in one gorgeous room after the next, and all of them sophisticated in a very different way than Worth Manor. He led her to the back of the house and a spacious sitting room that opened up into a garden. A walled, enclosed garden in the middle of London that said more about the kind of wealth Atlas possessed than anything else she could think of.

"Your house is beautiful," she told him honestly when he paused at the French doors, as if to make certain she was following him.

"It is," he agreed. Something moved over his face then.

"It was my pride and joy. A place like this was all I wanted from life and I achieved it when I was barely twenty-five, defying every person who told me that I would never amount to much. Of which there were a great many, you may be surprised to learn."

"I can't imagine anyone who met you would ever say something like that to you," she said before she thought better of it.

There was a curious, arrested look on his face then. "Don't worry, Lexi. I will have my revenge on them, too. There's more than enough to go around."

He opened the French doors then and she picked up her skirts and followed him out, down the stone stairs and into the spectacularly landscaped garden that managed to make the space feel as if it was far out in the countryside somewhere.

Atlas led her down a path that wound around through a bit of cheerful shrubbery before opening up on a little cottage that it took her a moment to realize was a pool house. And on the other side of it, a gleaming, deeply blue pool glinted in the afternoon light.

"Is this what all of this has been about?" Lexi asked, staring at the water, something tight at her throat. "Are you planning to drown me in your pool?"

She hadn't meant it the way it came out. She was trying to be lighthearted and she certainly hadn't meant to draw a direct line between herself, in this moment, and what so many people still believed he'd done to Philippa a decade before.

But when his eyes narrowed in response, she thought that maybe—just maybe—she'd meant exactly that, after all.

Then he smiled again, and it was worse.

Because she felt it everywhere, a dark, hot lick.

"The wedding was an act of revenge, it's true," he told her, in that soft, ferocious way of his that made her stomach flip over.

"I already know that."

"But it wasn't aimed at you. The wedding was for your uncle. Your cousins. Because I am certain they can think of nothing, collectively, more hideous than me as a member of their family."

Lexi started when he pulled her to him, those strong hands of his on her arms. Holding her there, directly in front of him, so that she couldn't have bolted even if she'd wanted to.

She told herself that of course she wanted to. Because she should. Because she did. Didn't she?

"What about me?" she asked. Though her voice was hardly more than a whisper and more than that, she thought she knew. She was terribly afraid she already knew. "What are you going to do to me?"

"I thought you understood." His thumbs moved then. This way. Then that. Sensation tumbled through her, a desperate kind of lightning, kicking up a new storm wherever it flashed. "I have a far more intimate revenge planned for you, little one. Over and over and over again."

"What if I don't want that?" But she hardly made a sound. Perhaps that was just the blood pumping too loud in her ears, drowning out the world. "What if I refuse?"

"Then refuse," he said.

He tugged her closer, and she should have made it harder. She should have made it hard at all, full stop. But instead, she went to him as if that was what she wanted all along. As if she'd been made to melt against him. As if this was why she'd stayed awake, restless and agitated, night after night...

"All you have to say is no, Lexi." Atlas held her against

him, and then he bent her back over his impossibly strong arm, making sure she was off balance. Making sure she could do nothing but cling to him. "I dare you."

And then he bent his head and took her mouth with his.

CHAPTER SEVEN

SHE WAS EXTRAORDINARY.

The taste of her exploded through him like some kind of roar.

He had brushed her mouth with his in the chapel, of course. The vicar had announced that he could kiss his bride, and he had. Barely. He'd leaned down, landed a businesslike kiss on her mouth, and it had all been over almost before it had begun.

There was no reason whatsoever that it should have haunted him ever since, as if there was much more between them than revenge.

But it had stayed with him, much as he'd tried to shrug it off during the wedding breakfast and reception. And now, here in his home at last, he finally—*finally*—took his time.

He took her mouth as if he owned her, because he did. Because he was finally part of the Worth family, whether they liked it or not, just as he'd planned.

And Lexi was his. Right now that seemed to matter a whole lot more than *plans*.

There was nothing halting about the way Atlas kissed her now. There was no fumbling, no haltingly fitting his mouth to hers and then figuring out how best to make it work. He simply claimed her.

His mouth opened over hers, possessive and greedy. As

if he'd been holding himself back all this time. As if he'd been longing for her, specifically, all these years. It was as if this was not a first kiss, but one of a great many. Thousands, perhaps. All of them exactly like this.

Hot. Languid.

Deep and rich and impossibly, inexpressibly lush.

And with every fierce, drugging pass of his mouth over hers, Atlas reminded himself that he did own her now. That she'd given herself to the barbarian returned to the family gate, and she'd known full well what she was getting into. He'd never pretended to be all that civilized before he'd gone to prison. And now... Atlas felt something savage beat in him like a drum.

He was a primitive man, when all was said and done. And whatever else happened in this dirty game, she was his.

Entirely his, to do with as he wished.

Her hands were in fists, gripping the front of his shirt. She fought, but not to get away from him. To get closer. As if all she wanted in all the world was *more*. His fingers speared into her hair, so soft and brown and pretty, and then he held her face where he wanted it.

And when he angled his head, it made everything slicker. Wetter. Hotter.

Even better than he could have imagined.

And Atlas had been in prison for a decade. He'd imagined everything.

At least two or three hundred times.

He kissed her and he kissed her. He indulged himself. He toyed with her. He tasted her. He was unapologetic and thorough at once.

And with every taste, every indulgence, Atlas felt.

He felt.

He, who hadn't felt a damned thing in years. He, who

had walled himself off to survive. He had become stone. Fury in human form.

But Lexi tasted like hope.

And Atlas couldn't seem to get enough. He couldn't seem to catch his breath.

He didn't want to think about revenge, not while he was losing himself in the sharp wonder of her kiss, and that alone should have made him let her go. Shove her away. Regain his equilibrium before he lost his mind completely—

But he didn't.

Atlas told himself it didn't matter what he felt. It mattered what he did.

And the woman who had locked him away and thrown out the key didn't deserve to know how greedy he was for her. She didn't need to know that he was very much afraid that he wasn't as in control of this as he should have been. She didn't have to know anything but this.

This.

The slide of her mouth beneath his. The carnal dance of his tongue over hers.

The sweet ache of her curvy little body in his arms.

If he couldn't recall ever wanting anything more than the next touch of her mouth to his, well. That was his cross to bear. She didn't need to know.

Lexi kissed him back as if she'd been waiting the whole of her life to taste Atlas like this. Exactly like this.

And he worried he would lose that tight grip on his own control for the first time in his life. Because it wasn't enough.

His body pressed against hers, his hardness against her softness, and that wasn't enough. His big hands tangled in her hair, then slid down the length of her back to cup her bottom and haul her closer to him—and that wasn't enough, either.

He kissed her again and again, and she met him with more of that reckless passion, and all the contradictory, complicated needs that spun around inside him nearly took him down to his knees—and that, too, wasn't enough.

Atlas felt possessive and entirely too wild, and everything he did to her made it worse. Because each and every one of her responses killed him.

Again and again, she killed him.

This was only a small part of his revenge, these moments with her. But for the first time, Atlas wasn't at all certain he would survive it.

And worse, in this moment, he wasn't sure he'd care if he didn't.

Something that should have sent ice down his back, but if it did, he was too far gone to care.

Atlas made a noise even he couldn't decipher, and then he was sweeping her up into his arms. She was nearly weightless, to his mind, and she smelled too good. Something soft that reminded him of the flowers his grandparents had grown on the island where he'd grown up, in those faraway sweet days that had been the only bright period in his early life. And had ended abruptly once his father had found him again and hauled him back to the slums of Patras in Western Greece, because he might not have wanted the child the wife he'd abused had run off to have in her parents' village but he didn't want anyone else to have Atlas, either.

He refused to acknowledge the memories, good or bad. Much less that enticing, tempting scent she wore. And yet he also didn't put her down and step away as he knew he should.

He wasn't sure he had it in him to step away. Not now he'd tasted her.

Atlas carried her across the terra-cotta pavers at their

feet. He laid her down on one of the soft, wide loungers that sat beneath the pool cottage's porch roof, right there on the edge of the pool. And he followed her down, stretching out above her and pressing her deep into the cushions.

The cushions were soft but she was softer. Atlas felt her body shift, as if to welcome him. To cushion him.

To wrap around him like a vine.

"This doesn't feel like revenge," she whispered in his ear, and she sounded drugged.

Or worse, hopeful.

Atlas laughed, though it was rusty and hurt a bit. "Oh, little one," he murmured, rough and harsh—the force of his desire too much to contain. And that sense of connection to her his business, easily shoved aside and ignored because he refused to indulge it. "I'm only just getting started."

"That's fine," Lexi said with a certain quiet directness that slammed through him. "I've been doing my penance all these years. I can handle your revenge."

"I'm delighted you think so," he replied.

And then he set his mouth to hers again, because it was easier. Or better. Or simply because he had to, or die wanting her.

It's not her, he growled at himself. *It's the fact she's a woman, that's all.*

He tasted her again, deeply, just to be sure. Because whether he liked it or did not, Atlas had lived like a monk for longer than seemed possible—even to him. Celibate asceticism had never appealed to him, but he had become what prison had made him. And the truth was he wasn't certain he even regretted it any longer. It was what it was and so was he.

It was prison that made her taste this good, he assured himself. It was the long drought that made her the sweetest, most perfect drink of water imaginable. He had been without for so long that he could hardly process that this was happening. That it was real. That she wasn't simply a product of the overactive imagination that had been his solace for a decade.

But she was here, right here, and she was a feast. The little noises she made in the back of her throat inflamed him, so greedy and delirious with need did she sound. It made him ache. It made him want more.

Lexi thrashed beneath him, and he wasn't sure why until he tilted back his head to get a better look at her face. And the answer slammed through him like some kind of cannonball, shot straight into him.

Need. She was wild with need.

And he couldn't seem to get enough of it. Of her.

The part of him that trusted no one, and her least of all, didn't trust this reaction, either.

But the rest of him—especially the hardest part of him—didn't care.

Because she tasted like magic and he had given up on magic a long, long time ago.

Because her hands tangled in his hair and tugged his face to hers, and he didn't have it in him to question that.

All Atlas knew was that he wanted more. Needed more.

As if, after surviving things that no man should be forced to bear, it would be little Lexi Haring who took him out. It would be this one shockingly pretty woman who would be the end of him. And not because she'd plotted against him, as he believed some if not all of her family had done, but because of this. Her surrender.

The endless, wondrous glory of her surrender.

It almost made him wish he was a different man.

He was tempted to rush. Just throw himself into her, into this, and glut himself until he was sated. He didn't know how he kept himself from it.

But he had waited so long. What was a little more self-control after all those years of keeping his nose clean? After managing, somehow, to keep from responding violently to all the seething brutality around him? After surviving, one day at a time, until all those days turned into years and eventually set him free?

So Atlas indulged himself. He told himself it wasn't her, specifically, but the truth was, he liked the fact that it was her. Specifically Lexi Haring, now Lexi Chariton. Now and forever his, her and whatever babies they would make together, and it was all the better that she brought the Worth family with her—

But Atlas wanted her, anyway. Worths or no Worths.

And the truth was, as he trailed his mouth down the length of her elegant neck and felt the fire of her pound through him, as he tasted his way across her delicate collarbone, he wasn't thinking about her family or her fortune at all.

He pulled the bodice of her wedding gown down, exposing her breasts to his view. He couldn't remember the last time he'd seen a pair of breasts so perfect. He doubted very much he ever had. Lexi's were high and perfectly rounded, as if they'd been shaped specifically to fill his palms. Her nipples were velvety, somewhere between rose and brown, and his mouth watered to taste them.

She arched her back, lifting herself toward him in wordless invitation, and Atlas remembered that this woman had married him. More than that, she'd kissed him back with all the ferocity he felt in his own battered soul.

So he bent his head and sucked one sweet nipple deep into his mouth.

Lexi was a marvel. She tasted better than she looked, which should have beggared belief. And he thought the sight of her—her head tossed back, her lips parted, her lithe and curvy body arched up to offer herself to him in the wedding gown he'd had made to suit her perfectly—would be branded into his head forever. As much a part of him as the things he'd suffered.

He suffered again now, though this was a far more tolerable agony.

She began to writhe beneath him, her breath coming in sharp little pants as he played with her perfect, sensitive breasts, and he reluctantly moved on. He wanted to strip her naked, so he could fully appreciate the gifts she was giving him and the full beauty of her surrender, but there was no time for that. She was laced in tight to her wedding gown, but he was a resourceful man.

He shifted to one side, taking her mouth again as he began to pull the great, voluminous white skirt up and out of his way.

And this time, she met his kisses with a deep, wild desperation that slammed into him like a kind of blow. He could feel it everywhere. In his sex. In the roar of blood in his ears, his veins, even his skin.

He thought his hands shook as he finally got beneath her wide skirt and found the satin of her flesh. He ran his hand up the length of one thigh, amazed at how responsive she was and how soft her skin was, as if he'd never touched a woman before in his life.

The truth was, though he knew he had, it was as if that was a dream from a different man's lifetime.

This was now. This was real.

Everything about this—about her—was new.

And then he found her heat.

Lexi was wearing the tiniest scrap of lace, so little it barely covered her mound. He stroked his way around the outside, pulling his mouth from hers as he bent his head to the task. And because that allowed him to hear her responses, gasps and moans, and more thrashing from side to side as if she couldn't contain herself.

She was like a wet dream, and Atlas felt like an adolescent all over again. He didn't want to wake up.

He learned her shape, cupping her in his palm and tracing the outline of her plump lips, then that fascinating furrow between them. And when the sounds she made tipped over into sheer nonsense, he found the edge of her panties and slid his fingers beneath.

And that was even better.

She was hot and she was wet, and he could smell her arousal. Molten to the touch, she lifted her hips to give him better access, and he took it.

Atlas found the center of her need, high and proud, and traced lazy circles around it as if he was learning a woman's body for the very first time. And he was. *Her* body.

Her responses. Her little trigger points. Her. *Lexi.*

He bent down to take her nipple in his mouth yet again and when he sucked her into his mouth, a little harder than strictly necessary, she rocked against him. So he twisted his fingers and drove deep into her welcoming heat.

And Lexi shattered.

She tensed and she shook, making high, keening sounds in the back of her throat, and he rode them out. His mouth and his hand, marveling as she came and came and came.

She was like a dream come true.

And she was his. Entirely and utterly his, to do with as he liked.

Revenge had never been so sweet. Sweet and hot and splayed open for his touch as if she craved nothing else but to lie beneath him just like this and come at his command.

It took her a while to subside. Atlas pulled his fingers from her clenching heat, and held her in the palm of his hand, reveling in her sweetness.

And so he felt the way she jolted when she finally opened her eyes.

"Oh," she said, her voice husky from all that crying out.

It washed over him like her hands on his body. All over his body, which needed to happen. And fast.

"Yes," he murmured, feeling uncharacteristically indulgent. *"Oh."*

"Well." Her tongue darted out to wet her lips. And even though he had his hand between her thighs already, that innocuous little gesture almost sent him over the edge like the adolescent she made him feel like. "That was... I don't know what that was."

"Do you not?"

She flushed. It was a charming shade of red, Atlas thought.

And it was more possible by the moment, something in him whispered, that she might be the death of him after all.

He shoved that aside. He was not going to be affected by this. By her. She was the one who would suffer here, not him.

Not ever again.

"Atlas..." she whispered, but whatever she meant to say, he didn't want to hear it.

This was about sex, nothing more. Not for him, anyway. There had been a time in his life when there was no woman he couldn't have seduced if he'd so chosen. He wanted that Atlas back. That version of himself, so bold and unafraid of everything after storming his way out of his father's clutches and into the life he wanted that he believed there were no horizons at all save the ones that marked the curve of the earth. No boundaries, no shackles. The world entirely his, and everyone in it, too, if he so chose.

He would have that Atlas back, or die trying.

And if he should happen to tear into glittering little

pieces the woman whose testimony had put him behind bars in the first place? Well, he wasn't exactly going to cry about that.

But he told himself he didn't much care if she did.

And he ignored the part of him that whispered that he lied.

"Quiet, little one," he growled, making himself sound even fiercer than he felt. "That was the easy part."

And then he showed her what he meant.

CHAPTER EIGHT

IT WAS LIKE a dream.

That was what Lexi told herself, though she knew she'd never had a dream like this. No dream could possibly have been so rich with detail. The scent of flowers and undefined greenery from the garden around them. The faint hint of chlorine from the pool. The sound of the water lapping against its sides.

And Atlas himself, who pulled away from her to stand there beside the pool lounger he'd laid her upon.

Lexi knew she should sit up. Cover herself. Do something as a nod toward the civility and good manners she was certain she'd had just a little while before.

But she couldn't seem to move.

Instead, she lay where she was and watched Atlas Chariton—*her husband*—undress.

She knew she should tell him the truth about her. About how inexperienced she really was—but she couldn't quite bring herself to do it. This didn't seem to be the place to talk about what it had been like these past ten years, with Philippa gone and nothing but grief and anger and Uncle Richard's expectations to smother her. How very little dating had appealed to her, anyway. How everything bright and good had seemed to die in that same pool with Philippa so long ago, and if that part of Lexi had died there, too, it had seemed a fair bargain.

And besides, he was a work of art.

She'd seen naked men before—on screen. But none of them were like Atlas.

She was hardly aware where he tossed his clothes, because all she could concentrate on was the glory of his intense masculinity, right there before her. It was as if all this time she'd been using the word *man* incorrectly.

Because as Atlas peeled off his elegant, obviously bespoke morning suit, she understood that he redefined the term.

Surely no one else had his particular combination of intensely sculpted shoulders, wide chest and narrow hips. Not like this. There was a dusting of dark hair over his pectoral muscles, and she couldn't seem to keep herself from following that line down, toward the part of him that was most fascinating, and most male.

"You look at me as if you have never seen a man before," Atlas said in that low voice of his she could feel echo inside her like heat.

Lexi flushed, the way she always seemed to do around him, and she didn't know how to handle this. Should she confess now? Or hope that she could hide her inexperience from him?

He stood there, the light of battle—and something much hotter—in his gaze. His mouth was curved in that dark, sardonic way of his that seemed wired directly to all that sensation deep in her belly. All of this felt like some kind of splendor, something magical that was only theirs, but she reminded herself that this was his revenge.

This was all revenge.

This might have been her wedding night. She might have felt more cared for, strangely, than she ever had in the past—but all that did was speak to the particular emptiness of her uncle's version of care. Because the truth was, there was nothing nice about this—or about Atlas. Nothing sweet. Nothing that was happening was about devotion or longing or all that wildfire she felt sloshing around inside her, and she needed to find a way not to be confused about that.

Because she was certain that Atlas would not be confused at all.

He was a man who'd had more lovers than anyone could count. Well did she remember the endless tabloid speculation into his private life, back when he was a self-made billionaire with his Belgravia house and that mind of his that corporations fought over, so intensely was his out-of-the-box business acumen celebrated. He'd graced the tabloids nightly with a different, usually famous, woman on his arm.

And he had only just gotten out of prison. It was safe to assume that he'd cut his particular sort of swathe across America on his way out of the country after he'd been released. It was also safe to assume this wedding night would be nothing to him other than what he had told her it would be, over and over.

Sex. Revenge. Penance, on her part.

But if this was penance, Lexi needed to spend more time on her knees—something she found alarmingly appealing when he stood over her like that, beautiful and brutal and focused on her as if there was nothing in the world for him but her. Only her.

All that sensation he'd wrought wound through her, still. She felt shattered. Ripped apart. Broken down into more pieces than she could possibly count, and she doubted very much she would ever put them all together again. Certainly not the way she'd been.

Lexi already felt changed. Permanently. She decided Atlas didn't deserve to know the truth about her on top of it. That would only make her vulnerable. Or more vulnerable, anyway.

She didn't think she could bear it.

So she held his gaze. She hoped hers looked defiant, not anxious.

"No," she told him, and made her tone as sarcastic as possible. "I've never laid eyes on a man before in all my life, Atlas. You're the first. The very first." She smiled, and made sure it was as sweet as it was sharp. "Congratulations. This was a white wedding after all."

The lethal twist in the corner of his mouth deepened.

"Of course," he said with an undercurrent of something that might have been laughter, had it been only a little bit softer. But it wasn't. He wasn't. "I should have known you would be into a little role-play, Lexi *mou*. Why am I not surprised?"

Lexi felt herself shake a little, amazed that it appeared she had pulled it off. That he thought she was joking.

She chose not to react to the part about role-playing, much less his sardonic tone, because she thought there were some things that didn't need to be debated while her breasts were bared to the London air. "Because I'm so resoundingly creative in all things?"

"I certainly thought so when you testified against me."

She knew she was supposed to feel exactly as she did, as if the wind had been knocked out of her. As if she'd fallen down flat on her back from some great height, and had to lie there in a panic, waiting to see if she would ever breathe again.

Lexi knew Atlas wanted her to feel that punch, that stunning wallop, and so she didn't react to it. Not visibly, anyway. She made herself smile. She stretched, there on that lounger, throwing her arms up over her head and arching her back a little as if she'd ever been that careless. As if she was as happy-go-lucky as Philippa had been, back then. And she knew instantly that it was the right thing to do when his gaze dropped to her breasts. And a look of wild hunger moved over his face, as if he couldn't help himself.

As if she had some power here, with him, after all.

It was amazing how much she wanted that to be true. If she couldn't have that connection her heart yearned for, even now, she'd take a little power.

Atlas took his time raising his gaze to hers again. And when he did, his black eyes were like flame.

"You appear to be overdressed, little one."

Lexi mimicked that lazy smile of his. She kept her arms tossed up above her head and she sprawled there on that lounger shamelessly, channeling Philippa in all her airy, blond ease.

"Then you should probably do something about that, shouldn't you?" she asked. As if she was someone else. Someone wild and free, the way Philippa had been, heedless and reckless and lit from within with all that light she carried with her.

Someone totally unlike the person Lexi had been for the past twenty-eight years of her life. First, she'd been a scared child, forced to grow up too fast in her parents' desperate, drug-addled home. Then she'd been the outsider in her uncle's family, made endlessly and repeatedly aware that she wasn't one of them and never could be. She'd been made to sleep in the servants' quarters, hidden away up under the eaves. She'd always, always been conscious of her lowly place beneath the rest of them.

But he didn't need to know about any of that, either. Not when she made herself languid. Light. The person she imagined she might have been, if things had been different long ago.

Atlas didn't seem to care if what he saw was real or not, which somehow made it all feel more real to Lexi. Instead, the expression on his face grew intent. Focused.

He moved over to her again, bent down and ran his hands down her sides. It was as if he was testing the fit of her gown, but then his hands gripped her hips and he flipped her over to her belly.

She felt her breath go out of her in a rush. Maybe she felt a little dizzy, too, from being spun about like that. Facedown on the lounger, she couldn't see him, but he left her in no doubt as to where he was. His hands were everywhere. She felt them in her hair, and only realized what he was doing—that faint little bit of pressure, a tug here, there—when he tossed the gleaming clip that had held back her curls onto the cushion beside her face. Then she felt his calloused fingertips track over her exposed shoulder blades before she felt him get to work on the intricately laced back of her wedding gown.

She thought she should say something. Toss out something suitably sophisticated. Offhanded. Something that would really make him believe that she was as experienced as she was pretending to be. Or at all. But she couldn't seem to force words past the constriction in her throat. Or through the wild swirl of heat that licked all over her body, swirling around and around, inside and out, until it knotted into something spiked and hard and infinitely hotter, deep in her gut.

The only noise was the water splashing down into the pool from the fountains that fed into it. It was as if they were all alone in the world, with only her elevated heartbeat in her ears and the sound of her ragged breathing, amplified by the cushion in front of her face.

And Atlas was like some kind of shadow above her and all around her, his hands against her skin every time he opened another wedge in her gown. He moved quickly, determinedly, working his way down her spine button by button, hook by hook. And somehow, every button he pulled loose felt like a caress.

And then it really was a caress when he moved over her, stretching out above her so he could press his mouth to each bit of her back that he revealed.

Lexi's eyes drifted shut. Her lips parted and she couldn't seem to make them close again. Because she couldn't seem to pull in a deep enough breath, and some part of her didn't want to. She wanted to stay in this endless, red-hot tumble of his hands, his mouth, the exquisite heat and weight of his body pressing against hers from behind. She could feel the soft, satiny sweep of her gown beneath her, falling to each side as he opened the back a little wider.

And then he was shifting her again, one hand moving beneath her to hold her up as he tugged and tugged the fabric out from beneath her body.

She opened her eyes to see the great cloud of white settle on the stones beside her. And even as she felt Atlas come back down over her again, her heart kicked at her. Because if she could see her dress, that meant that she was, for all intents and purposes, naked beneath him.

In the next beat of her thundering heart, she had no doubt about that. Because she could feel him. Everywhere. He stretched himself over her like some kind of cat, and then bore her down with him.

And God help her, but she'd never felt anything better.

She thought, perhaps, that this was what dying felt like. That wild, heedless, reckless descent into too much sensation to bear. His chest pressed against the slope of her back. She could feel how hard he was, which made her feel softer.

She melted; she could feel that melting as if she was a piece of metal he'd held over the fire, and oh, how she glowed.

He put his mouth to the back of her neck, and did something with his tongue that made her mind go blank. While everything else...tightened.

It was delicious. It was delirious.

Or perhaps she was.

One strong, impossibly hard arm snaked around her middle and then hauled her tighter against him. He turned then, holding her tight against him as he moved them both to their sides, and then cradled her there in his arms. She felt his big, hair-roughened thigh press between hers. Her head lolled against his huge, muscled arm as if she could no longer lift it of her own volition while his mouth performed lethal acts against the line of her neck.

And then, impossibly, she would have said, he found her mouth.

Everything was dark, and hot, and a new kind of insanity that Lexi wasn't entirely certain she could survive.

She wasn't sure she cared either way.

And that was when she felt his hand smooth down the front of her. He tested the weight of one breast, then the other. He used his palm to test the shape of her nipples, massaging her until they stood at attention. Then he moved on, finding her navel and then smoothing his way farther down until he reached the edge of the lacy pair of panties she still wore. This time, he didn't hesitate. He was finished playing around.

He slid his hand beneath the fabric and found the center of her need in the next instant. And Lexi would have said that it might take a while to build her back up into the same keening sort of fire as before, but it turned out she knew very little about her own body. Or at least, what Atlas could do to it.

Because all it took was the expert slide of his blunt, hardened fingers against the most tender part of her, and she was thrown, sprawling, straight back into the fire.

He muttered something against her mouth, releasing her lips, then dropped his head so that his mouth was against her neck. He tested the shape of her heat once, then again, then he said something else, dark and low and possibly in Greek besides.

But she understood him, even though she didn't know the words. She understood that this was sex. Dark and wild and dangerous.

His hand moved, she felt a sharp tug—

And she only realized that he was tearing her panties from her body when he was finished.

And she knew better than to exult in it. It was a show of brute force, nothing more. And besides, she knew perfectly well he'd done it deliberately.

To remind her.

But she didn't need reminding. She didn't know why instead of terrifying her, or upsetting her, all it did was make her tremble. Desperate for more.

Desperate for him.

He smoothed his hand over her thigh, pushing the leg that was higher forward, and out. She let him arrange her, because that felt good, too, in the same way that all of this felt good, as if she was balanced on the edge of a knife and no matter which way she fell, she could expect to be sliced deep. Changed forever. Scarred, most likely.

But if there was something in her that was meant to care about that, she couldn't access it.

And then she felt it. Him. The large, satiny head of his manhood there against her entrance. Her breath came faster and she could hear the faintest high-pitched sound she made with each one.

Atlas laughed, and it was like a shudder working its way through her, unlocking deep reservoirs of need that she'd had no idea existed within her.

He surged against her, pressing the wide head of his hardness against the place where she was softest. Wettest. Hottest.

She was fiercely, suddenly, surpassingly glad that her face was turned away from him then. Because the sensation was too much. The fact that he was holding her in such an awkward position—one leg up, completely surrounded by his body, one hundred percent trapped and controlled in his grip—overwhelmed her. She could feel too much. She could feel everything. She could feel things and places she'd never paid any attention to before, and each and every sensation was wilder than the one before.

She thought she might have stopped him, if she could have seen what he was doing. If she could have seen *him*. If he hadn't been so determined and inexhaustible as he pushed into her. Not particularly fast, not particularly hard, but ruthless all the same.

She expected something to tear, the way she'd read in a thousand books. She thought she'd feel a ripping, some kind of sundering from deep within, but it felt more like a disconcertingly intimate pinch. Then a dull, heavy sort of ache. And he couldn't see her face, so she let herself react to it. She screwed her eyes shut and she pressed her mouth against the cushion beneath her, so no sound could possibly emerge.

And still he pressed into her. Deeper and deeper.

So deep she expected him to hit bottom, but instead, he filled her.

Deep. Wide.

Impossible.

She had never felt anything like it in her life. Nothing

could have prepared her for this. No books, no movies, no late-night television shows, could possibly have made her ready. Because there was no music swelling around them. No cunning soundtrack to set the mood.

There was only flesh. Hers and his. There was his strength, all around her, hard muscle and the inexorable slide of his penetration. She could smell him, a hint of sandalwood and citrus and man, that inflamed her senses as she felt the different textures of his body. The rough smattering of hair on his thighs, his chest, against her. The smoothness of his heated skin where there was no hair. The steel bars of his arms around her, and that granite chest of his pressed like a wall to her back.

It was as if she was a doll he could move as he liked, and she didn't know why that notion should make a kind of lightning storm dance throughout her body. But it did.

And then he was inside her. So deep he only stopped when she could feel the hard head of his flesh flush against her. She felt stuffed. Impossibly, uncomfortably full.

Of him.

"Are you okay, little one?" he asked, and he sounded different than he had before. Something like shaken, she would have said—

But that didn't make sense. And she could feel the thickness in her throat. Something like a sob in her chest, because it hurt. It ached. It was a dull, spreading heat that her body couldn't quite process—

Lexi thought she would die before she'd let him know. She would die before she let him see her in pain. Hurt. Flayed wide open, like this.

Because she knew it was what he wanted.

"Never better," she gritted out, her mouth against the cushions.

He shifted behind her, and that hand of his that had

moved to her thigh to help guide his entrance drifted back between her thighs.

And Lexi had to bite her own tongue to keep herself from crying out as he ran his fingers through her softness again.

She couldn't process the sensation. She couldn't handle it. She felt split wide open, and yet his hand was on that needy, greedy part of her. For a moment she stiffened, as if her body planned to buck him off her no matter what it was she thought she wanted. She could even feel moisture in the corners of her eyes, then tipping over to leave tracks down her cheeks—

But she refused to break. She refused to surrender.

Lexi refused to give him this when she'd given him everything else.

So instead of trying to push him off her, to alleviate the pressure in the stretching and that intense fullness, she began to move. She shifted her hips from side to side, then worked her body in little, terrified circles, attempting to do something—anything—about that ache. She felt more than heard his sharp exhalation.

She would have stopped, worried that she was doing something wrong or even hurting him, but just as she started to change what she was doing she felt a little bit of that heaviness ease. Though it was more complicated than that. It changed. The pressure began to feel like heat.

So she moved a little more. This way, then that. Until she found a way to rotate her hips that allowed her to feel the length of him. She could pull away a little bit, then push back, and that felt like fire.

And then it felt far, far better than fire.

"You're killing me," Atlas gritted out at her ear.

And then he took control.

And Lexi was inordinately grateful that she'd worked

a little bit to shift that intense ache into something infinitely hotter and all-consuming, because Atlas gave her no quarter.

He held her tight against him; he pinched that proud little button between her legs between his fingers, and then he began to move.

And with each stroke, that slick retreat and then the insane, deep thrust inside her, he blew her mind.

Atlas taught her things she didn't know how to name.

He turned her inside out, he tied her into knots and then he taught her the difference between the little bit of heat and a blazing, uncontrollable fire.

And he did it again and again and again.

Just as he'd promised.

And the world fell away. Revenge and lust disappeared, drawn into all that flame. Need and fear, loneliness and hope; everything burned.

It was like a baptism, encompassing and total, and Lexi lost herself. She tumbled, heedless and ecstatic, into the crazy inferno he created between them with every deep, shuddering stroke. It was as if there were no boundaries between them. As if they were one—dark and wild, hot and greedy, moving together in a delirious concert that some part of Lexi never wanted to end.

And this time, when he threw her over the edge, it was hard and fast, like an explosion rather than the slower shattering before. She arched, and thought she screamed, and then he was pulling out of her while everything inside her pulled too tight, then hummed red.

She was capable of little more than a wordless sound of complaint, but then she was on her back and he was coming down over her again, wedging himself between her thighs and then pounding into her all over again.

And it was even more intense this way.

Deeper. Harder.

And she never quite came out of that explosion. It went on and on, as he gathered her beneath him and slammed into her. It was beautiful and it was mad, inspiring her to lift her hips to meet each thrust.

Again and again and again.

And when she fell apart this time she screamed loud enough that she had no doubt what noise she'd made. And she heard him roar out her name, right there against the side of her neck, as he followed.

And it was astonishing how much she wanted to believe that this could be something more than it was. That what they'd just done could be real.

Real, not revenge.

When she knew better. Of course she knew better.

But for a moment, as he crushed her beneath him, still lodged deep inside her, Lexi forgot that she was a Worth, and Atlas was the man pledged to destroy them all. She forgot to remind herself that this was what happened when a passionate man had been locked up for years and had nothing to do with her.

She forgot to keep herself safe.

Instead, she held on to the man who was her husband no matter how they'd come to say their vows, and she pretended—with everything she was and a thousand dreams she hadn't known she harbored deep within her—that this was real.

That they were.

That the only man she'd ever loved might possibly feel the same way about her.

CHAPTER NINE

LEXI WAS DAZED through and through.

She was aware that Atlas pulled out of her and that he removed his significant, delicious weight from on top of her, but she drifted off again. After a while—though she couldn't have said how long—she became gradually aware of her own harsh breathing. Sometime after that, she realized she was curled up in a ball, naked, still lying on that lounger beside the pool.

But she kept her eyes closed, because Lexi had no idea how to function when she felt so profoundly changed.

Altered from the inside out.

She hadn't expected that sex would be like this. So... all-encompassing. That it would take her over. That *he* would. That it would sweep over her and through her, making her feel as if even her skin was new. As if she would never be the Lexi she'd been before this had happened, not really. Not ever again.

And the strangest part was how little that notion upset her.

She heard a faint movement and opened her eyes to find Atlas settling down on the lounger beside her, so that she rolled slightly into his side. She wanted to push herself away—maybe *because* she didn't want that at all. Because she liked touching him. More than liked it.

Touching him, even when the touching was secondary, made her feel something like whole.

Not that she had the slightest idea what *whole* felt like. But she didn't roll away from him.

And then she regretted that choice when something about the intent way Atlas's gaze tracked over her face made her self-conscious. Lexi started to move, but his stern expression stopped her. She lay there instead, holding her breath, as he reached over and dragged one thumb beneath her eye.

It came away wet. Atlas stared at the moisture on his thumb, then shifted that arrested, accusatory stare to her.

"It has been a while, I grant you," he began, and she didn't want to hear that particular knowledge in his voice. That certainty. She didn't want to see it in his black gaze.

"I'm sure you glutted yourself on every available woman you could find the minute you stepped out of jail," Lexi threw at him, because she felt defensive. And the best thing for that was a good offense, apparently.

"I would have liked nothing more than to glut myself silly," Atlas said, a kind of foreboding in his voice. "But I had other concerns. So my memory of such things goes back a dusty, desperate decade. And yet…" His arrogant brows rose then, convicting her where she lay. "I am waiting for you to tell me that I imagined it."

"Imagined what?" she ventured.

"I will tell you this once again," he said in a lethal tone that made her flush. "I cannot abide lies. Whether of omission or directly to my face. I abhor them. I will not tolerate them. You would do well to remember that, wife."

"You haven't asked me a question," Lexi replied, hoping she sounded much less cowed than she felt. "How could I possibly have lied?"

She hated that she was naked, suddenly. She shoved

herself up into a sitting position. Wiping at her face, she pushed herself back against the tilted headboard of the lounger to get away from him. She had the fleeting thought that she should get to her feet—but she let go of it in the next instant. Because Atlas was huge and hard and dangerous and she could tell by that severe look on his face that he had no intention of letting her put any farther distance between them.

Which made her chest feel tight. Swollen, somehow. She pulled her knees to her chest and tried to convince herself that was adequate armor.

"You have approximately three seconds to come clean," he growled at her.

"Everything with you is theater," she threw back at him. "If you already know, why make this into a spectacle?"

"Two seconds."

She scowled at him. "I don't think it's necessary for you to try to intimidate me."

"One second, Lexi." His cruel mouth twisted. "And I'm not trying to intimidate you. You should be intimidated already. It should be like a great, heavy stone, pressing you deep into the ground. And as you gasp for breath, little girl, you should contemplate exactly what it is you did that led us here."

She breathed in, then out. She did not gasp. And she told herself there was no damned stone.

"Yes, Atlas," she made herself say, fighting to sound somewhere between matter-of-fact and offhanded and not at all sure where she'd ended up. "I was a virgin. Are you satisfied?"

If anything, her confirmation made his face go darker. There was a kind of storm in that dark black gaze of his— and Lexi hated that he was right. That it felt like a stone after all, parked square on her chest and crushing the air from her lungs.

"How the hell did that happen?"

His voice was a low, accusing growl, and his scowl was ferocious. It should have made her melt into a puddle, but instead she sat a little straighter. After all, she was already naked. Literally stripped. What was a little more vulnerability?

"Virginity?" she asked tautly. "Well, Atlas, perhaps you forgot while locked away from the world for so long, but that's really more about something *not* happening."

His jaw worked. "I would advise you to think very carefully about attempting to be cute."

"I'll tell you a little story, shall I?" Lexi asked, pretending that warning tone of his didn't bite at her.

All of this was uncharted ground. She felt torn apart, literally. She could still feel him, deep inside her, in that place no one else had ever gone. The place she had hardly known was even there. She felt...frazzled and altered and changed beyond recognition. She felt the hard prickle of tears threatening behind her eyes, and the very notion that she might cry in front of him—actual sobs, not whatever had happened before when she'd been out of her head—appalled her. Her breathing was uneven, her breasts ached, and she still felt a leftover sense of fullness.

But all that shattering had left her insides...jumbled. It made her bold. Or unconcerned, anyway, with the consequences of voicing the things she would ordinarily swallow down.

"Once upon a time there was a little girl named Lexi," she told him, glaring at him as if he didn't frighten her at all. "When she was eight years old, she was saved from a nasty little house that was filled with junkies by her very kind and grand uncle. Ten years after that, the only friend she had in the world was killed." She pulled in a breath when Atlas shifted as if he meant to comment on that. "Or died. It's all very unclear."

"People drown." Atlas's words were like bullets. His gaze was worse. "It was only made unclear when you testified that a conversation you'd eavesdropped on and took out of context made me a murderer."

That took the wind out of her, but she made herself ignore it. "That's not the story I'm telling."

Atlas's dark eyes blazed. "Why ever not? You told it so well ten years ago that you took away a decade of my life."

She had tried apologizing to him in the carriage house. She didn't bother to try again, not when he was looking at her as if he wanted to take her apart—and not the way he just had, with sex. She pushed on.

"During those same ten years, the little girl we're talking about felt that she had no choice but to try to take the place of the friend and cousin she'd lost," Lexi said quietly, holding Atlas's harsh, accusing glare with her own steady gaze. "She made herself the perfect daughter, though she had no father. She made herself the most dependable sister in the world, although she had no brothers. She worked overtime in the family business, though she was never, ever, allowed to imagine herself a part of the family."

She'd meant it all to come out sharp. Edgy. But instead, there was that sickness in her throat again and too much emotion in her words. Still, there was no stopping now. She tilted her chin and refused to look away from the big, brawny man glaring at her. The man who had been *inside* her.

The man she had recklessly, foolishly married.

"And shockingly," she said in the same quiet, intent voice, "in all that time, trying to live two lives at once and do both so well that it would somehow make up for what had been lost, our heroine had absolutely no time to date."

Atlas only studied her for much too long, as if she was a specimen beneath a microscope.

"You are not required to date someone in order to get laid, Lexi," he said, horribly, and only after Lexi's ears had started to burn. "Have you never heard of a one-night stand?"

"My bad," she said. Through her teeth. "I knew there was something I was neglecting all this time."

"I thought you told me you were a whore."

She lifted her chin farther and tried to ignore all the dark, heavy things that turned over inside her at that. "I feel like one now. I assume that was the plan."

If he had been another man, she might have described the expression on his face then as…lost. And she almost dared hope that she might have reached the man she remembered, buried down deep inside him—

But this was Atlas. There was nothing lost about him. As if to underscore that, he stood and she drank him in despite herself, as if his uncompromising male beauty had nothing to do with the way he was stirring her up inside. As if they were unconnected, when she knew the real tragedy was that they were all part and parcel of the same thing. Of him.

She had been a virgin, he was the only man she'd ever touched and she didn't see how she could possibly be expected to keep herself from staring at that part of him that had so recently been deep inside her.

He was still somewhat hard, and so big, she felt her eyes widen even as a new heat wound its way through her.

"This changes nothing," Atlas said, and there was a note of finality in his voice that made her steel herself as she looked up. Up and then up farther, because he was so tall and dark, beautiful and remote.

The way he looked down at her then hurt. And Lexi didn't think she could handle it another moment, not stripped and exposed the way she was. She reached down and grabbed the first thing she could find on the ground beside the lounger. Her wedding dress. She pulled it up and over her, covering herself in all that soft, sweetly airy fabric, because she couldn't bear his too-dark eyes on her naked body another moment more.

"I'm glad you think so," she said, and her voice was still thick, though she fought to keep it even. "I'm sure that's true for you. But I don't think you get to decide what this does or doesn't change in me."

"I don't care what changes in you," he told her coldly. So coldly. After all the heat, all the fire, it felt as if he'd hauled off and slapped her.

Lexi had no doubt that it was deliberate. That this was Atlas putting her in her place, definitively.

And she hated herself for letting it hurt her.

But more, she finally understood the contours of his particular revenge against her in a way she never had before. How he would use her, how he would tear her into so many pieces she would never be able to put herself back together, and what, exactly, that would do to her.

He'd called it an intimate revenge, and on some level she was glad that she'd had no idea what that meant. Because if she had, would she have been able to go through with the wedding? Or would she have run away instead of subjecting herself to this?

She didn't know. She didn't know anything, it turned out.

Except one thing.

He could never know the truth about her feelings for him. That she'd never had a girlish crush on him. That it had always been so much more.

Not ever.

"You want to destroy me," she whispered.

And she hated herself more when it came out as a kind of query.

Atlas only stood there, looking down at her. He was entirely pitiless. Merciless. Steel and stone, and nothing but darkness all over his harsh face. She could see it as if it was stamped all over his skin.

"Yes, Lexi," he said quietly. Resolutely. "I thought you understood. When I'm finished with you, there will be nothing left."

"Atlas…"

"Nothing," he said again, even more softly this time. "I am your husband. You stood before God and your uncle and made it so. And I vow to you, I will be the end of you. Piece by piece, Lexi. Until nothing remains."

"Atlas," she said again, aware that she was showing too much then. She was showing him everything. "You must know that I never meant to hurt you. I only told them what I saw. What I heard."

Slowly, very slowly, his cruel mouth kicked up in one corner. And Lexi felt her stomach go bottomless as she realized, with a sickening sort of lurch, that she was giving him exactly what he wanted.

"I promise you this," he told her, with that dark current of satisfaction kicking through his stern tone and obvious in his black gaze. "There is no penance that you can pay that will clear your debt to me. Though I will let you try, Lexi *mou*. I will let you try and try and try. And the more you try the harsher it will feel. The worse it will get. And the more you will wish you never, ever dared think you could betray me and escape unscathed."

She found she was gripping the material of her wedding dress in her fists.

"Unscathed?" she whispered, too shell-shocked to scream. Too unsteady to move, for fear her legs wouldn't hold her if she tried to stand. "Do you truly believe that any of us escaped at all, much less *unscathed*?"

"Remind me where you were incarcerated."

"I don't pretend to understand what it was like to spend all that time in prison," Lexi managed to say. "But you're not the only one who suffered. And in case you wondered—and not that you've asked—living here for the past ten years wasn't exactly a walk in the park, either."

"I'm sure your suffering was great indeed," Atlas said, with dismissive contempt he did very little to conceal. "But unless you were in a cell all this time, I will somehow refrain from weeping salty tears on your behalf."

"It's not a competition. You have no idea what my life has been like."

"I don't care."

The simple, ruthless ferocity of that took her breath away. Lexi fell quiet, and the smile that Atlas aimed at her then was little more than a baring of his teeth.

As if he was a wolf, plain and simple.

What Lexi couldn't understand was how she'd thought otherwise. For even a second.

Or what she was supposed to do now with her poor, bruised heart.

"Welcome to your new life, little one," Atlas said harshly. "I hope it hurts."

And then he left her there.

In pieces.

Just as he'd promised.

CHAPTER TEN

SHE DIDN'T BREAK.

Atlas went hard on Lexi over the next weeks, because he hated the part of him that had tasted her and thought that ought to have given her immunity from what she'd done. Or worse, forgiveness.

He was appalled. And he gave her no quarter.

He moved her from her carriage house office into the sleek wing of the manor that served as the Worth Trust headquarters, installing her in the office opposite his so he could watch her through the glass walls. And better yet, catch her watching him.

By day, he treated her like an employee. And he was a much kinder boss than he was a husband.

Because by night, he treated her like she was his. As if she'd been placed on this earth for no other reason but to please him.

Another man might have called it a honeymoon. He took her everywhere. In his car. In every room of his house. Again and again in the bed they shared, until she was slumped over him and dead to the world.

He took her so many times he might have called her a compulsion if he didn't already have a far better word at the ready. *Revenge.*

It was revenge when he made her ride him until she

sobbed. It was revenge when he reached for her in the night, desperate to get inside her again. It was revenge when he showered with her in the mornings, the soap slick on her skin and too much a temptation to resist. He never did.

He kept telling himself it was revenge, because that was the only thing he could allow it to be.

Revenge was why he was here. Revenge was the only reason he had married her. Revenge was the only explanation he would accept.

During the day, he held that line. It was even easy. He'd rolled back into the Worth Trust, and all the trappings of his old life, with precious little resistance. Atlas knew what that meant. He knew that it was deeply unlikely that Richard Worth would so easily hand over the reins to his own empire if he wasn't afraid of what might happen if he did not.

But there was no point in issuing accusations when he had nothing but his knowledge of Richard as evidence. Not yet, anyway.

It was easier to let time go on. To gather evidence as he went, bit by bit. Closing that noose on his own time, in his own way.

While he waited for the inevitable knife in his back once again.

And in the light of day, it was easy enough to see Lexi as the enemy he knew—*he knew*—she was.

In the dark, things got messy. Alone in his house, he was only a man and she the woman he couldn't seem to keep his hands off.

"I'm not a doll," she told him on one of those evenings, when he'd been unable to keep from sampling her in the car on the drive home, and so was charmingly flushed as he led her into one of the lower reception rooms. He'd had the staff arrange the new wardrobe that he'd had made for her in the room, so that it looked a great deal like the couture house where he had her wedding gown made. Dresses here. Actual power suits there. Accessories on every surface. "I can dress myself just fine all on my own, thank you."

And at the beginning of this, he thought, her voice would have been sharper when she said something like that. More brittle. But she had changed, too, in these weeks together. She was softer now. More yielding in all the ways he liked best.

Even at times like now, when she was frowning at him, her arms crossed and her back too straight.

"You are my wife," he told her, as if that fact might have escaped her mind today. "Left to your own devices, you are free to dress as you wish. Why exactly you wish to dress like a very sad office worker who has an inbred distaste for fine fabric, I do not know. But it does not matter." He nodded toward the chic, sophisticated clothing that graced every surface. "I wish my wife to dress like this."

"You realize, I assume, that everything you just said is offensive. Insulting, even."

"Toughen up, Lexi *mou*," he suggested idly, though he never shifted his gaze from her for a moment. "Or you will never survive this."

"I thought that was the point," she said, and something turned over inside him at the sight of that flash of something too dark to be heat or temper in her gaze. It looked a lot more like hurt, and he hated the fact that it got to him. And that it was becoming harder and harder to pretend that it didn't. That she didn't get to him more and more all the time. Especially at night when all his carefully plotted revenge fantasies seemed a bit too far away. "It's going to be hard to grind me down into dust beneath your feet if I'm tough enough to survive the impact."

He reached for her then, because his mouth on hers was far more eloquent than he could be. Because his hands against her skin whispered all the truths he least wanted to face.

Because the night was a liar and he refused to let it make him one, too.

And every morning he rededicated himself to the notion that all of this was nothing more than the revenge he'd craved for too long. That the signs he was getting to her were good. That he felt nothing.

Least of all, shame. Or that far more worrisome urge to protect her from everything, even himself.

Meanwhile, Atlas fended off the rest of the decidedly unhappy Worth family with significantly more glee.

Gerard was the only one among them who wasn't entirely useless. Atlas allowed him to stay on in his marketing role, and took pleasure in the fact that the eldest Worth was required to report to him.

Too much pleasure, perhaps.

Other members of the family weren't as lucky.

"You can't fire me," Harry blustered at him one fine morning. It was nearly two months since his wedding, and Atlas was feeling charitable.

It had everything to do with the way his beautiful wife had knelt down on the shower floor that morning and taken him into her mouth, making him groan out his release so loudly it had echoed back from the tiles. It was the only reason he had allowed this meeting to take place, in fact. He'd been feeling so relaxed and at his ease that he'd actually allowed Harry to come and sit in his office, rather than simply sending security to escort him from the building.

"And yet," he said, watching the other man's face redden, "I think you will find that I can. And am."

"But I am a Worth! This place is made out of my blood!"

"Which is the only reason, I imagine, anyone allowed you into this office in the first place." Atlas shrugged. "You didn't work for me ten years ago, Harry. I can't imagine why you think you should work for me now when you have done so little in the interim."

"You bastard—"

"If I were you," Atlas said, his voice stern and frigid, and God-knew-what expression on his face, "I would take my seat before I put you back in it. With force."

Harry started, as if he didn't realize he'd risen in the first place.

"Damn you," he growled at Atlas after a moment. As if he was collecting his thoughts. "Where does it end with you? Wasn't it enough that you did whatever you did to Philippa? Must you torture the rest of us too?"

"Do you actually know what exonerated means?"

"It has to be you," Harry threw at him.

There was something different about the way he said that, and it took Atlas a long beat to realize that he wasn't drunk. Or at least, not obviously so. Atlas thought it was the first time he'd seen the other man sober since his return.

"It has to be you," Harry repeated. "Because no one else was there."

"Except your cousin," Atlas supplied. "Are you suggesting that my wife murdered your sister?"

Harry ran his hands over his face. "Of course not."

"Much as I know you enjoy blaming her for all the ills of this family, I think you will find that she, too, has an alibi. Do you?"

Harry looked genuinely startled. "I didn't kill my own sister."

"Neither did I." Atlas lifted a brow. "She was choked. There is no debate about it. Choked and then dropped into the pool on the off chance she might have lived through the choking. The only thing that ever put me there was Lexi's testimony. Otherwise, I feel certain the witnesses who saw me in the village would have sufficed to get me off. There is such a thing as physical evidence, after all."

"I don't know why you're telling me this. I know this."

"Are you certain? Because you seem to be in some doubt. Again."

"It has to be you," Harry said again, but there was no temper behind his words. No red-faced insistence. If anything, the younger man looked sad.

But Atlas refused to feel sorry for him. Or any of them. That way led to nothing but madness. And, no doubt, a stint in another prison the moment he let his guard down.

"And the fact that you believe I am a killer despite all evidence to the contrary," Atlas said smoothly, "is why I cannot have you in this office. You understand."

"I am Harry Worth," Harry sputtered. "I have worked for the family—"

"But you see, that is the problem. You do not work at all." Atlas shook his head. "In some ways, I pity you. You never had a chance. But then I remember that you have a hefty trust fund. You could live off the interest for the rest of your life. What that means is that there is no reason whatsoever for me to tolerate you. I can raise my own children to do what you do here, and far better."

Harry blinked, but it wasn't his hurt feelings that got to Atlas. "What am I supposed to do?"

Atlas only stared back at him, expressionless. "That is not my problem."

And he wasn't particularly surprised to find Richard in his office again, a few hours later.

"How do you suppose it looks when you fire one of

my sons from their own family business?" the older man demanded.

This part, Atlas enjoyed. "I can't say that I care."

"Well, you ought to care. This sort of bloodletting makes it look like you have something to hide."

"Does it?" Atlas asked, letting his gaze slam into Richard. And he liked it when the old man's eyes narrowed. "Or does it look as if I am finally cleaning out my closets?"

But the truth was, firing Harry didn't sit as well with him as he might have hoped. It wasn't as satisfying as he'd imagined it would be. It was good business, certainly. As far as he could tell, Harry had never worked a full day in his life. He'd treated Worth Trust as an extension of his swinging bachelor lifestyle, at best. He'd sauntered in sometime in the afternoons, sat at his desk doing God knew what for a couple of hours, and had spent the rest of his time attending the various galas that the family was invited to as wealthy members of British high society. That was it.

There was no reason that Atlas should have felt at all concerned about the decision he'd made. There was certainly no reason that it should have felt anything but victorious to rid himself of one more Worth. One more thorn in his side plucked, he told himself stoutly. That was all.

"I thought you wanted this to be about family," Lexi said that same night, sitting rigidly beside him in the back of the car. They were on their way to a charity event, which was the only reason Atlas hadn't already worked out the strange feelings that sloshed around inside him all over her delectable bottom.

"I am nothing if not a family man," Atlas told her, his tone deeply sardonic. "As you will discover when we start our own."

He hadn't discussed that part of his plan with her, but he suspected she already knew. After all, she might have been a virgin but she'd never been stupid. And he'd yet to use protection.

"Everyone knows that Harry is a liability," she said quietly. He glanced at her, but Lexi's gaze was aimed out the window as London slipped past. He thought she sounded sad herself, and it clawed at him—but then he reminded himself that he wanted her that way. That it was part of the plan, that was all. "But I don't think there's any situation in which firing one of the two remaining Worth brothers makes you look anything but vindictive."

He took her hand in his, and told himself he was trying to intimidate her. That was why he toyed with her fingers, one by one. Intimidation.

"I am vindictive."

"Of course. But I'm not sure there's any benefit to *looking* that way in the eyes of the entire world."

"Are you defending Harry? When he has done nothing his whole life save bully you?"

"*Bully* is a strong word."

"My mistake. I'm sure that when he called you the hired help he meant it in a loving way."

She looked at him then. And he didn't understand why that cool stare of hers seemed to pierce him to the bone. "Harry is who Harry is."

"A drunken lout, you mean. All red nose and belligerence."

She lifted one shoulder, then dropped it. "Do you really want to operate on his level?"

That ate at him. But he couldn't address it again unless he admitted it bothered him—and that would never do.

Atlas Chariton did not feel. He was forged from fire and rage and he liked it that way. He refused to feel any guilt, any shame, any shred of concern that he was becoming the very thing he had hated himself, years back.

He refused to let himself feel anything at all.

But then he found himself out on the dance floor in the middle of a dreary waltz, surrounded by the sorts of stuffily dressed people who had applauded when he'd been arrested, and would likely do so again were the police to show up tonight and haul him away. A month ago he would have found that notion cheering. Tonight he didn't—but he couldn't think about that. He was meant to thrive on opposition, after all. Not find that after all this, he was tired of it.

This is madness, he snapped at himself. *What the hell is happening to you?*

He focused on his wife instead.

There was something different about her tonight, though he couldn't quite put his finger on what it was. There was something softer about her face, perhaps. It was as if she glowed, though he could see that she hadn't done anything different with her cosmetics. Her hand was warm in his, so he focused on that. He swept her about the floor, not at all surprised to find that she was an excellent dancer, smoothing out his roughness with the easy perfection of her steps.

Even if she did insist on keeping her gaze trained somewhere over his shoulder.

Defiantly, he thought.

"What is different about you?" he asked, his voice low, when she'd managed to ignore him—even as she danced in his arms—for the whole of one song. He didn't let her go as the next began.

And he felt her pulse leap. He narrowed his gaze, trying to read her face, but she only glanced at him briefly before she looked away again, and her expression remained composed. Cool. Impenetrable.

"Different in what way?" she asked mildly, as if they were discussing the chances of rain tonight. And this was

England. The chances were always high. "I've recently married. Perhaps you've heard."

"How very droll. That is not what I meant, as I think you know."

"I was also recently a virgin," she said, in the same distantly polite tone. "Perhaps that's what you see. Do I get to be a whore now?"

It was astonishing, Atlas reflected, how little he liked that word when she used it.

"I think not."

This time when she met his gaze, she held it.

"Tell me why that is," she urged him, a glint in her brown gaze he didn't care for. "Because the only man I've slept with is you? Or because married women, by definition, can't be whores? Or, I know. There are some innate anti-whore protections inside me that only you see."

He said nothing for a long moment, and didn't like the tightening sensation in his chest. "This is a strange attempt at defiance, Lexi. Is this an argument you truly wish to win?"

"I think that's a very good question," she replied, and held his gaze while she said it. "And one you may want to ask yourself one of these days. Before it's too late."

"I don't know what you mean."

"Do you not?" He felt her hand clench tight around his for an instant, before she released it. And there was that *something* he couldn't define again. She seemed brighter, somehow. And that didn't make sense. Brighter and softer, and yet she was looking at him with something he was tempted to call desperation. "What happens if you win, Atlas? What if you get every single thing you want? What then?"

"Then I win." He gazed at her in a kind of arrogant astonishment. "That is the goal, after all."

"And then what?"

"Haven't we covered this? After you have all suffered for eleven years, I will entertain the notion that you might have paid your debt. But not before."

"But what does that look like?" Her voice was fierce and it seemed to connect too hard to that part of him that he refused to call guilty. Or ashamed. "Do you require actual blood? Shame? A public flogging or two? I'm trying to understand where the line is."

"Wherever I say it is."

She pressed her lips together. "So I am to be punished by sex, forever."

He laughed at that, and he liked that sensation a lot better. "I am not certain that anyone who comes as often as you do can rightly call that punishment."

"You know that Harry is ineffectual at best," she said, from between her teeth. And it took Atlas a moment to realize that she seemed genuinely agitated. "He's drunk all the time and often provoking, certainly. The reality is that he's nothing but a sad man with few prospects and too much money. He's not a worthy adversary for you, Atlas. But that didn't stop you from crushing him."

"I would hardly call relieving the man of a job he didn't value *crushing him*."

"Of course it crushed him," she hissed at him, as if she couldn't believe he'd said that. "His contribution to the Worth Trust might not have been meaningful to you, but it was the only thing he had."

"I'm astounded by this compassion," Atlas said acidly. "Such deep concern for someone who has evinced nothing in that vein for you. Ever."

"Would a little compassion kill you?" she demanded.

He stopped moving. Just held her there in the middle of the dance floor, and for once he didn't much care who watched them or what they thought. He only cared that this woman—his wife—was looking at him as if she was disappointed in him.

Not like he was her worst nightmare come to life. He was used to that. This was worse. This made him *feel*. All those messy, impossible things he kept assuring himself he couldn't feel. He wouldn't feel.

He thought some part of him might hate her for it.

"Since when do you care what happens to Harry?" he demanded, under his breath, because he was afraid that if he spoke any louder he would shout down every chandelier in the place.

"I don't." Her voice was much too tight. As tense as the rest of her. As tense, perhaps, as he was. "I'm just trying to establish a baseline. Is there any member of this family you won't try to grind beneath your heel? Are Gerard's children safe from your wrath? Is anyone?"

"You should worry a little less about them and a little more about you."

He watched her chest rise, then fall, betraying her agitation.

"I'll take that as a no," she whispered.

And Atlas should have felt that like yet another victory. One more triumph to add to the list.

But instead he felt uneasy. He couldn't put his finger on why.

Lexi pulled away from him, then swept off to the powder room, and when she emerged she was far more docile. She made charming party conversation wherever she went. She posed for photographs. She smiled; she laughed.

But Atlas didn't believe it.

Later that night, he made her scream. He secured her hands above her head on that wide bed they shared. And he kept her on the edge for a long, long time. He made her sob over and over. He made her call out his name, until it sounded like yet another cry.

He threw her over that edge, again and again. He made her beg, plead. It was pretty and she was nothing short of magnificent, but it still wasn't enough.

Nothing was ever enough.

It was revenge and it could never be anything *but* revenge, Atlas told himself as he lost himself inside her. As he poured himself into her. As he gathered her to him and then started all over again.

As if he was the one paying penance.

And he didn't think much of it when she told him she felt off the following day. A headache, she told him when she stayed in bed instead of joining him in the shower, that she was certain would go away if she babied herself a little bit.

He allowed it. A time to regroup and have a rethink, he thought.

But when he arrived home that evening, she was gone.

And it wasn't until the hour grew late that he realized she wasn't coming back.

That she'd actually dared leave him, for good. Taking nothing he'd given her, he discovered in short order. Just the things she'd come with. Some of her old clothes. A few books. Nothing else.

And he thought that was the worst of it. Her betrayal. Her reckless attempt to evade her just desserts—until one of the maids came before him the following morning as he was preparing to launch a full-scale response that he was certain his wife would not enjoy at all.

"I just thought you should know, sir," the woman told him, shaking with what Atlas imagined were nerves.

"Know what?" he asked, trying not to sound as short-tempered as he felt.

"We found it in the bin in one of the guest room toilets," the woman managed to say. "And we wouldn't have looked through the trash, of course, but it fell out when we were emptying the bins."

Atlas tried to summon his patience. "What fell out?"

"This."

The woman held out her hand with something in it, and it took Atlas entirely too long to register what it was. What it meant.

Because he wasn't sure he could take it in. Because it looked entirely too much like...

He blinked.

No. It was impossible.

But the woman before him didn't waver. She kept her hand extended, and that meant he had no choice but to stare at the object she held.

It was a pregnancy test. One of those sticks with a window at one end, featuring a large, unmistakable blue cross.

"It's a pregnancy test, sir," the maid told him, in case he was still in doubt about what had happened. That Lexi had actually gotten pregnant, welding them together in a new way and linking his own blood to the Worths, forever, just as he'd wanted. And then left him without sharing this news. "And you have my congratulations, sir. It's positive."

CHAPTER ELEVEN

LEXI HADN'T BEEN to Martha's Vineyard in years.

Ten years, to be precise. She'd left after Atlas's conviction and she'd never imagined she'd return. She'd never *wanted* to return to the place that loomed in her memory so painfully, swollen with the ghosts and memories of that final summer and everything that had happened since.

But the truth was that she hadn't necessarily wanted any of the things that had happened to her over the past two months.

That didn't mean they were all entirely unwelcome. Her hand crept over her belly as she drove her rental car from the ferry port at Vineyard Haven toward Edgartown, and she felt certain she could feel a slight roundness there already. A thickness, anyway. A tiny indication of the life within.

Discovering that she was pregnant had changed everything.

It had all happened so fast that night after the charity ball. She'd suspected something was off for at least the previous week. She'd bolted upright while it was still dark outside and crept into one of the guest bathrooms on a different floor of the house, so that Atlas would have no idea what she was up to even if he woke to find her missing from their bed. She'd followed the directions to the letter though her hands shook, afraid that if she deviated even the slightest bit it would invalidate the whole thing.

And then, a few minutes later, there it was. Proof in blue lines that her life would never, ever be the same.

The strange, dull headache she'd been having off and on made sense, then. That odd, insatiable and yet specific hunger, that veered too quickly into something heavier and closer to ill. The strangest sensation of thickness, everywhere.

She was pregnant.

And as Lexi stood there, the test in one hand and nothing around her but the silence of Atlas's house in the early morning, it was as if the tumult of the last weeks crystallized there before her. She'd thrown the test in the trash, even covered it with extra toilet paper to keep it hidden from prying eyes, but her mind hadn't been whirling in a panic. She hadn't been feverishly searching for a way to react to this news through a sea of shock.

It was as if she'd already known. As if the test was a moment of clarity—a confirmation—nothing more.

But the clarity was what she needed. It spurred her into action.

She'd moved quickly, because Atlas was a light sleeper and she'd expected him to wake and find her missing at any moment. She'd padded through the house, but had gone downstairs instead of back to the master bedroom. She'd found her laptop in the library where she'd left it, and bought herself a one-way ticket to Boston, leaving later that same morning. It seemed obvious that Massachusetts was the last place on earth any member of the Worth family should ever want to go, so it stood to reason that it was the last place on earth anyone would think to look for her, too.

And when she was done she'd walked back upstairs, slid

back into the bed where Atlas sprawled like the Titan he was named for. She'd even drifted back to sleep for a while.

Her dreams had been chaotic. Bright colors and intense emotion. All the things that had been whirling around inside her that she'd been afraid to look at directly. Love. Loss. And that endless ache for things that could not be.

Atlas had woken her up again a few hours later the way he always did, and she hated the fact that this was still so hard, clarity or no. That there was such a huge part of her that didn't want to accept what she knew was true. That Atlas was incapable of feeling the things she did. That prison had excised that part of him or maybe it had never been there.

Lexi knew who he was. She lived in his house, under his thumb. She'd worked with him every day since their wedding. She knew how he thought, how he reacted, how he considered things from all angles and went in for the kill. More than that, she knew him in every intimate way possible. There was no part of her body that he hadn't explored with his hands, his lips, his tongue and his teeth. Not to mention that other, more dangerous part of him.

She had explored him in the same way despite the fact he'd told her again and again that the only end to any of this was her own destruction. It was as if she couldn't help herself. Not when destruction felt so good. So right.

What Lexi couldn't understand was how he could catch at her the way he did. Even the morning she planned to leave him. She sometimes thought she loved him most in these in-between times. The early mornings, or late at night, when his black eyes were softer, somehow. When he hadn't been awake long enough to sink back into his revenge. His strategies. His plots.

He was a different man looking back at her than the one she knew him to be in those moments. The man she'd always imagined he was, not the one she'd learned he truly was. Maybe it was no wonder that her poor heart was so confused.

But that day, she finally found the steel inside her that had been missing all this time.

She said what she needed to say to get him to let her stay behind. And once he left for work, she sprang out of bed, threw the few things that were hers into a bag and ran out of that gleaming white house as if she expected him to be lying in wait for her somewhere in the garden square.

He wasn't, of course.

And once she'd made it away from Atlas's street, walking briskly toward the Sloane Square tube stop, Lexi had to face the part of her that had hoped, deep down inside, that he'd seen through her. That had expected him to appear and claim her, keep her going, even beg her to stay—

Childish fantasies, she knew. This had all been about revenge. He'd told her so from the start.

It was her own fault that she'd fallen in love with him so long ago and couldn't seem to stop.

She didn't bother to let any of her relatives know that she was leaving England—and her job, her family, her life—with no plans to return. There was no point pretending any longer that they had the slightest interest in her as a person. As a human. As long as they could get away with treating her like something far, far beneath them, that was what they'd done. And anything that happened now that was less condescending, thanks to Atlas's interference, was on sufferance.

They were her relatives. Her blood, she supposed. But she was going to have a baby now and she was determined that her child would have a family.

A real family.

And if that family was necessarily small, if it meant

only Lexi, well. She would make certain, with her last dying breath if necessary, that her baby never had cause to believe that it was anything but perfect.

What shocked her the most was how easy it all was to walk away.

You could have walked away at any time, that sharp voice inside scoffed at her as the Piccadilly Line train swept her into Heathrow Airport. *The moment you left school, for example. Anytime in the past ten years. Before that wedding. But you didn't want that, did you?*

And the truth was, there was a large part of her that didn't want to get on that plane. That wanted to turn around, go back to Atlas's house and pretend she'd never tried to leave him. That thought a little more time, a little more love, might save them both.

But she knew better.

Lexi had gotten on the plane. She'd flown over the ocean the way she'd done so many times before, but never alone. She'd rented a car in Boston and had driven out to Cape Cod where she'd spent the night in a cozy, gray-shingled bed-and-breakfast a block or two from the water, and the following morning she'd taken the ferry to Martha's Vineyard.

The island was as beautiful as she remembered it. More so, perhaps. It was a beautiful late-spring day and she could see the sea as she drove, blue and slumbering in all directions. She soaked it in. And when she finally arrived at Oyster House, pulling open the gates to let herself in and closing them behind her again with the same old combination that had been on the gates when she was a child, she understood why she'd come here.

The baby that grew inside her even now was the future. But in order to give her child everything it deserved, Lexi had to find a way to let go of the past.

Of course she'd come here, she'd thought as she pulled up near the grand old house that sprawled on its bluff above the water. Because until she found a way to come to terms with what had happened here eleven years ago, she would be stuck forever. She'd be just like the rest of them—just like Atlas—running around and around in ever-tightening circles, and never going anywhere.

The trouble was, she didn't know how to break that cycle.

She spent the first night huddled up in a ball in the empty, shut-up-tight house that no one had set foot in for a decade. It was dusty, echoing. Strange, when she remembered it with the windows open and the sun streaming in, filled with life and Philippa's laughter. The electricity had been turned off, but that didn't stop her. She'd walked through the empty rooms with an old flashlight she'd found in the kitchen, staring at the indistinct masses of covered furniture as if each shape before her eyes was its own ghost.

She slept in a room on the third floor, just beneath the widow's walk, that Philippa and she had shared all those summers. It was a funny little room, with a long, narrow hall and a strange, separated shape, so each of them could feel as if they slept alone while sharing the same overall space. They'd called it their summer camp.

And it was possible, Lexi thought that first night, that it was only here—camped out with all those memories she'd kept at bay for a decade—that she allowed herself to accept the truth.

Which wasn't that she missed Philippa, though she did. Oh, how she missed her. But there was a darker truth beneath it. One she'd never told a soul.

Lexi had been furious with Philippa the night she'd died. Hurt. Jealous.

It made her feel like a monster.

Here, now, all these years later, she lay in her old bed and stared out the windows at the stars.

"I'm sorry, Philippa," she whispered out loud.

She rested her palms on her belly and apologized to her lost cousin in her head. Because her first reaction when she'd found Philippa in that pool had been shock. Terror. Anguish, certainly.

But sooner than she liked to admit, she'd remembered the conversation she'd overheard Philippa having with Atlas, and that was where she failed her cousin. Her only friend in the world.

Because even then, eighteen and awkward and aware that she was destined for a life in the shadows instead of Philippa's preferred spotlight, Lexi had been jealous. Wildly, surpassingly jealous that Philippa—or so the conversation she'd overheard had suggested had some kind of relationship with the man Lexi had loved so foolishly for so long.

Maybe if she'd been more forthcoming from the start, the police and detectives could have found the real killer. Maybe if she hadn't been so obsessed with Atlas, she wouldn't have waited to tell her uncle what she'd heard. Maybe if she'd been better to Philippa, if she'd loved her cousin and best friend more than her own hurt feelings, she could have prevented all of this. Instead of running away when she'd heard that sharp conversation near the pool, she could have strolled right out. Sat down and joined in.

And maybe today, Philippa would be alive.

She hadn't done that. Lexi had been too busy nursing her poor, wounded heart and crying into her pillow, and now look at what had become of them all.

Was Lexi the reason that Philippa's killer was still out there?

Lexi couldn't say for certain. But huddled there in that room that reminded her of all the happiest moments of her childhood as well as the worst, she tried her best to make her peace with what she hadn't done.

The next day, she walked the grounds. She let the sea and the sun soothe her from all sides. More than that, she let herself talk to the ghosts that followed her everywhere she went. The memories, sweet and painful in turn. One way or another, she was determined; she would close this book and move on.

If she couldn't do it for Philippa, or herself, she needed to do it for her baby. She knew that.

But on the third day, as she walked near the overgrown garden that sloped down the long lawn that rolled from the house on the bluff down to the sea—her senses filled with the scent of summer green, blackberry bushes and tomato plants, wildflowers and a thousand memories—she felt the strangest prickle of awareness wash over her skin.

And when she looked up, as if she'd conjured him from the depths of her broken heart, Atlas was there.

Lexi told herself she had to be hallucinating. That this was just another one of the dreams that woke her in the night, so real she was sure she could reach out and touch him...but he was never there.

She blinked, but he didn't disappear. He stood there as the wind washed over the both of them, as if it was a caress. She could smell the rough salt of the sea in the distance. There was the particular Martha's Vineyard cocktail of sweet green grass, privet hedges in full bloom and beach plums. There were blue hydrangeas against the weathered gray of the house, the endless blue sky and Atlas in the center of everything as if he'd been propping it all up on his shoulders all this time.

He looked dark and grim and entirely too beautiful,

very much as if she'd conjured him out of her wildest fantasies. A little bit windswept, that dark black hair of his in all directions. More shocking, he wore a pair of dark, casual trousers low on his narrow hips and a thin T-shirt that hugged his athletic, sculpted chest like a lover. No three-piece suit tailored to his specifications, corporate and sleek. And yet somehow, to her eyes, he looked even more powerful than usual.

"How did you find me?" she asked softly.

For a moment she thought the breeze stole her words away, tossing them down the length of the overgrown lawn into teeth of the rising tide, but no. She could see he'd heard her. His beautiful head tilted slightly to one side as he regarded her.

As if he was biting back his temper.

Deep inside, something in Lexi turned over. Then shuddered.

"There is one thing you should know," he said, and he sounded different. Harsher, somehow. Rougher. "I will always find you. There is no place on this earth that you can hide from me, Lexi. That should have been obvious."

"What's obvious is that I will have to find a better way to leave you, then." She lifted her chin. "Because unless you lock me in a cell, Atlas, I am leaving you. I've already left."

"That will never happen," he told her, his words ringing out like a bell.

He moved toward her then, and as he closed the distance between them, Lexi's heart kicked at her. Hard. Her palms felt clammy and there were goose bumps marching up and down her arms. Because he hardly looked like himself. He looked...wild.

Unhinged, she might have said, if he was someone else. If he was someone other than Atlas Chariton, a man carved from the coldest, heaviest stone and solid rock all the way through.

"Tell me," he said as he came closer, every word a bite, "what of my child?"

Lexi flinched at that.

"Oh, yes, my deceitful little wife," Atlas growled at her, his gaze as black as night. "I know."

CHAPTER TWELVE

Lexi swallowed then. Her own legs felt precarious beneath her. There was a riot inside her, but she did her best to ignore it. She concentrated on Atlas instead.

Atlas, whom she'd never really seen before, she thought. Not like this.

"Is that why you came here?" she asked. "One more opportunity for you to stake your claim?"

"And why not?" He was too close now. And it was as if she was swept up in his intensity without his having to lay a single finger on her. That brooding masculinity that enveloped her where she stood. "Can a man not claim his own child?"

"*My* child," she threw at him. "And no, you cannot claim it. You cannot have it. You have more than enough pawns already. More than enough chess pieces to sling around your board until you crush them all. You don't need this child, as well."

He laughed, though not in a way that suggested he found anything amusing. Then he pressed the fingers of one hand between his eyes. She had the sense he was holding back his rage. Literally.

"You cannot possibly imagine that I will allow you to keep my own child away from me," he said, cold and harsh.

And something inside Lexi broke then. Or perhaps it

had already been broken. Perhaps she was the one who had been in pieces, all this time, until a pregnancy test healed her.

Because suddenly, it was as if she was a different person altogether. One who was no longer afraid. One who was not cowed, or intimidated. Not by the generations of Worths who had stood exactly where she did now and had somehow produced her uncle, who had gone to such lengths to keep her in the dark about who she really was. And what was hers. And certainly not by this man who had married her and torn her apart, night after night, while doing his best to give her absolutely nothing of himself.

But Lexi was tired of *nothing*.

"Look where we are," she threw at him, her voice hard. Because she had nothing left to lose. Or more to the point, there was nothing she wanted from him. Not one thing.

Because the only thing she would ever want from him was something he was incapable of giving anyone.

She knew that now. She told herself she accepted it.

"The poetry of the moment has not escaped me," Atlas retorted.

"I'm glad you find it poetic. I find it sad." She threw out a hand without meaning to, as if her fingers could encompass the whole of the house above them, the sea below. "It's as if time stopped. Eleven years ago we were all thrust into a nightmare and there we've remained, ever since."

She closed that last bit of distance between them then, and she didn't think. She reached over and poked Atlas Chariton in the chest. And then she did it again, simply because she could. Because his arrogant astonishment no longer fazed her.

Because what could he possibly do to her that he hadn't already done?

"I will not raise a child in this horror show," she told

him, with a solemn sort of matter-of-factness. "I've had enough. There's no more penance left to give. Forgive me or don't, I don't care. You can have all the money I never knew I had. I don't care about that, either."

"Are you above that, too?" he asked. Not at all nicely. "What a saint you are, Lexi. A proper martyr."

"Why would I want it?" she asked, perhaps a little wildly. "It has blood all over it. My mother died because of that money. Philippa died because of that money. You went to prison for a decade because of that money. Do you know what I want from that money?" She shook her head at him. "To be free of it, once and for all. And all the twisted, bent, terrible people who come along with it."

"How lovely it must be for you," Atlas replied, tense and low, "up there on your high horse."

"I don't want this." Lexi threw the words at him as if she thought they might hurt him. "I want no part of it."

Of you, she didn't say. But his face froze as if he heard her, anyway.

"My heart bleeds for you, truly," Atlas gritted out. "But I am afraid I cannot accommodate you. You are my wife. You carry my child. Neither one of those things is something you can run away from."

"Why do you want me at all?" Lexi asked, her voice a bit more jagged than she would have liked. But she couldn't let herself worry about such things. Not now. "Your revenge is complete. You've taken over your old job and made it clear to anyone who knows you that you're back and in full command of your little empire. You got what I imagine must have been enormous pleasure out of firing Harry, who will likely drink himself to death in short order. You've made Gerard feel maligned and passed over. Better still, you've ruined Lady Susan's plans for world domination by reducing the fortune she thought she was marrying into by a significant amount. My uncle no doubt lies awake each night, horrified unto his soul by all of this, but most especially, as you pointed out, the fact you are now related to him by marriage. What else is there?"

His cruel mouth twisted. "I told you. Eleven years of suffering."

"The past two months have been nothing if not eleven years of suffering packed into each and every night."

"Funny," Atlas drawled, that terrible heat in his black gaze. "That is not the impression I get, every night, when you sob out my name as if I am a deity."

"I've been in love with you for the whole of my life." Lexi hadn't meant to say that, much less shout it at him, but it didn't matter. There was no need to pretend any longer. Not now, when everything was over. When all of this had finally gone too far. "And even now, even though you told me who you were and what you wanted, I imagined that it could all be different. That some part of this would matter to you. But it doesn't. It can't. Because the only thing you care about is your own damned pride."

"What did you say?"

He sounded almost strangled. But Lexi charged on.

"Yes," she hurled at him. "I said your pride. That's what this is about, and don't you try to fool yourself that it's something else. Your pride is hurt. And I don't blame you. Nobody blames you. I can't imagine what it would be like to go through what you've been through, and I have no idea how you go about getting past that. But this whole plot of yours? To take everything? To make us all pay and pay and pay?" She shook her head, suddenly aware that she was perilously close to tipping over into a sob. "Philippa was my friend. I loved her. She was the only person in this world who loved me back, and she died alone and afraid. Do you know why?"

"Because somebody killed her. And I think you know who. I think, deep down, you've always known. I know I have."

"This isn't about your detective skills, Atlas," Lexi snapped. "She died alone because I let her. Because I heard her having an intense conversation with you about your relationship, and it hurt me." She pressed her palm against her own chest and dug the heel of her hand in, hard. "And I will never forgive myself for my spiteful, angry little heart. For the fact I ran away and hid like a pouting child. That I didn't look for her earlier, when she didn't return. That I left her out there all night long. What would have happened if I'd walked out and revealed myself in the middle of your fight?"

"You have been misunderstanding that conversation for eleven years," Atlas roared at her, but the volume didn't scare her. That intensity on his face didn't scare her. She was too far past that now. She felt reckless. Bullet-proof, somehow, after these admissions. "There was nothing between Philippa and me. Ever. Except your uncle's dreams of a tidy little dynasty he could control. Do you know what we were arguing about that night?"

"Yes. She broke off your relationship and you—"

"There was no relationship, Lexi," Atlas growled. "Your uncle wanted an arranged marriage. But Philippa refused. And yes, I was furious with her. I always knew that as long as I was an outsider, that could be used against me. I always knew that marriage was my way in. I couldn't think of a single reason she would say no. But she could."

"Like what?" Lexi asked, hearing that ragged edge in her own throat, revealing her in ways she was sure she wouldn't like when she felt steadier. But it was taking her over, from the inside out, whether she liked it or not. Because she couldn't think of a single reason anyone could refuse Atlas.

She hadn't, after all, and she'd known full well that he was marrying her for his own nefarious reasons.

"You hid and listened, did you not? You already know."

She did know. She'd been astonished and furious when she'd heard Philippa say it, because it hadn't made any kind of sense to her. Atlas had offered Philippa every single thing Lexi had thought she wanted.

"She said she didn't love you."

Atlas nodded. "I thought she was having a laugh. What the hell does love have to do with anything?"

It was like a hard blow, directly into her gut. It took the fire and fury out of her as if he'd kicked out her knees.

"And that," she said quietly, "is why I cannot be around you any longer, Atlas. I just can't."

Something in him seemed to break, right there in front of her as she watched. His dark eyes blazed with something too dark, too stormy, to be pure temper. But the look that moved over his face then was more like...anguish.

"How convenient," he gritted out as if the words were torn from him. "Such a deep, abiding love this is, Lexi. I only hear of it when it is gone, held forever over my head, always out of reach. Are you sure that *love* is the word you should use to describe such a thing?"

"I have always loved you!" She shouted it at him, not caring if she was getting loud. Not caring if all the island heard her, though she knew they wouldn't. There was nothing for miles but the sky, that perfect robin's egg blue. The sea down at the bottom of the rolling lawn, keeping its own secrets, and seagulls floating lazily on the breeze high above.

"You love the idea of me, if that. I make you come again and again, that's all. I think perhaps you've confused sex for love. It happens, you'll find. Especially to virgins who don't know any better."

"Don't you dare dismiss the things I feel!"

"Is this what you call love?" Atlas demanded, opening his hands wide as if he was waiting for the world to answer him, not just her. "You've never spoken of it. You've never given the slightest hint. Instead, you run away from me. You do your best to steal my own child away from me, without any intention of telling me it existed in the first place. This is what love is to you? And you dare to stand here before me and act as if I'm the one with problems?"

"I'm not the one who's dedicated my life to some insane revenge plan!"

Atlas reached over and wrapped his hands around her shoulders, hauling her closer to him. "And what do you call this if not revenge, Lexi? Do you really dare to stand before me and claim this is anything other than an attempt to hurt me in kind?"

And all the fight went out of Lexi then, in a kind of spiral. If he'd let go of her, she thought she might have reeled back in a kind of shock.

But he didn't let go.

"I have never pretended to be a good man," he told her, his voice as urgent as it was dark, and the look in his eyes matched. "But I am a man of my word. I do not lie, Lexi. I have never lied to you."

"Congratulations," she said, though she was no longer throwing the words at him like bullets. "You promised me nothing but pain, Atlas. And I believed you."

"Tell me what I have done to you that is so heinous," he growled at her, leaning down to put his face in hers. "Tell me what I have done to deserve this."

"You…"

"I hurt your feelings," Atlas answered for her. "And in

return for this, you decided to conceal your pregnancy, leave the country and to act as if I left you no other choice."

"Was I given any choices?" Lexi asked, feeling heart-sick and broken, all at the same time. And yet she didn't push away from him. On the contrary, there was that part of her that thrilled to his touch, even now. Even here. Even when all of this was over. "You made it perfectly clear that I was not."

"I said a lot of things," Atlas growled at her. "And yet every night, there I was, punishing you with a thousand orgasms. Oh, yes, you've been used terribly. How you must have suffered. Again and again and again."

"I apologize that I somehow failed to psychically dis-cern the true meaning behind all the sex," Lexi retorted, feeling stung and off balance, which only upset her more. "As you pointed out, I was a virgin when you married me. This is the only sex I've ever had." She tipped her chin up. "For all I know, it's all like this."

His laugh was hollow and dark, and he gripped her a little more intently. "If all sex was like this, Lexi *mou*, the world would be a different place."

"I can't read your mind, Atlas."

"Ask me for what you want," he suggested, sounding as raw as he looked. "Ask *someone* for *something* that you actually want, little one. Or do you still not know how?"

Because he knew, she realized then, that she never had. That she'd learned long ago that there was no point asking for the things she wanted, because nobody cared if she got them. Nobody cared about her at all.

The only one who had was Philippa, and look how Lexi had repaid her.

"Fine," she said now. She pulled in a breath and she held his gaze as proudly as she could. "Love me, Atlas. Is that what you want to hear? Because that's what I want." He only stared back at her, raw and unreadable, and so she forged on. "I don't want your revenge sex. I don't want a thousand orgasms to make me suffer. I want you. I want a real marriage, made of hopes and dreams instead of evil plots to take down your enemies. I want to raise this baby together, and not in shame. I want to heal. But most of all I want you to love me." She let out the breath she'd been holding in a rush. "And you can't."

His grip on her shoulders was harder then, his fingers digging into her skin, but she didn't mind. He looked tortured. Outside himself.

And she didn't know how to keep herself from *wanting*. From wanting to help him. From wanting to touch him. From wanting him, full stop.

"I don't know how," he threw at her, like some kind of howl had been ripped out from the deepest part of him. "Don't you understand that? You speak of love, but I don't know how."

And she did love him. Still. Always. She took no joy whatsoever in watching him suffer.

"Atlas," she began, lifting her hands to brace them against his wide chest. "You can't—"

"My father was an abusive drunk," he told her, as if he couldn't stop himself. "I never had anyone else in this world except the grandparents he took me from when I was five. When I was finally old enough to break away from him and go find them again, they had died." He shook his head as if the memory still haunted him. "I have never had anything in this world except the things I made with my own hands, or my brain, or whatever other tools I found inside me. You say the only person who ever loved you died here eleven years ago. And some part of me is envious of that, even though I know what happened, because I never had even that."

"Atlas, you don't have to—"

"This was supposed to be easy," he hurled at her. Very much as if he was issuing accusations. "I wanted to hate you, but you made that impossible. And I can't forgive it. I can't get past it." He shook her slightly, just enough to make her breath catch. "I can't find it in me to make you pay."

"I've already paid," she whispered.

"I don't want your penance, Lexi. I want you."

"You want to hurt me, you mean."

"Hurting people is the only thing I know how to do." Atlas said that so quietly. So hopelessly. His hands dropped from her shoulders then and Lexi felt it like a blow. "I have nothing else in me. I know why you ran. I would have run, too. But I told you, I am not a good man." His grave, stern face was ruthless, pitiless. But his black eyes gleamed with what Lexi was afraid to let herself believe might be emotion. "I may not know how to keep you the way you deserve, but I also have no idea how to let you go. I can't."

"Atlas…"

But he didn't stop. It was as if, now he'd started, he couldn't.

"I don't know how to love you," he told her. "I don't know how to love anything. But I know this. When I discovered that you left me, I was furious, but it was still the same game. I still wanted to play it. But when I found out you were pregnant…" He shook his head. "It changed everything."

"It should change everything," Lexi said fiercely. She slid her hands over her stomach as if she could already feel their child kicking in there. "This is the future, Atlas. Not the past. This is a baby, not a ghost. And our child deserves to be loved. Cherished. Cared for."

All that dark, terrible anguish seemed to wash over him then. "I don't know how to do that."

And Lexi's heart cracked wide open.

She knew he was right. She'd called what she felt for him *love* even as she'd left. Even as she'd run away, planning never to return.

But love was about forgiveness, not fear. Love was yielding and tough in turn. Love did not quail at the first sight of trouble. Or even eleven long years of it. Love could be embattled. Armored. It didn't have to make sense.

But there was no pretending that love meant leaving. There was no pretending that she'd been loving anyone but herself, and her old fantasies of who he ought to have been, until now.

And how could she stand here and hold him to a higher standard? When she didn't ask the same of herself?

"I don't know how, either," she said when she thought she could speak over that aching thing in her chest. "How could anyone know?"

"Stay with me," he said, his beautiful face ravaged. Even his cruel mouth twisted into something tortured. As if he'd never been made of stone at all. "Stay with me, and I will learn. I am a man who has done everything I ever said I would. I have been a legend in my own time repeatedly. I learned how to run multinational companies when I grew up in claustrophobic slums. I can do anything I put my mind to, I know it. Stay with me, and I will dedicate myself to learning how to love you, and this child, with all that I am. All that I have. All that I'll ever become. This I promise you."

And everything in Lexi wanted to believe him then. More than she had ever wanted to believe anything.

She could hardly get the words out. "If this is your real revenge…"

"I can't sleep without you, woman!" he bellowed at her then. Atlas Chariton, undone. "You are all I think about.

You make me regret the man that I have become, and wish, with all that I am, that I might be a better one. All I wanted was revenge, but all I see is you."

And Lexi realized that her own vision was blurry. That she couldn't seem to keep the tears at bay any longer.

But Atlas wasn't finished. "Is that love? I do not have any way of knowing. But I know this." He reached over and traced an abstract pattern over the line of her jaw. "You are the only thing that has made me smile as long as I can recall. The idea of you carrying my child makes me feel like a god among men. And I cannot imagine a life that does not have you in it." He moved that hand to her chin and held it, the way he had a lifetime ago in her carriage house office. When he'd threatened her with everything she'd always wanted. "Stay with me, little one. And we will teach each other how to love. Until it is as natural as breathing. You and me and this child we made."

And maybe, Lexi thought, love was faith, in the end.

The belief that whatever had gone before was less important than what might come and more, the strength to step forward instead of forever turning back.

The belief that fighting for more, not settling for less, was worth it—no matter how painful the fight might be.

She had tried to be like steel. Hard. Ruthless. And all it had given her were tears and ghosts in an empty house locked up tight against ten years of winters and a lifetime of terrible memories.

Instead, she could try yielding. Softness.

Love, no matter what. No matter how much it scared her. No matter how vulnerable and exposed it made her feel.

"I love you, too, Atlas," she said, with soft conviction. "I always have and I always will."

And she was the one who stepped to him, then. She

slid her arms around his lean, hard waist, and she tipped back her head so she could look him full in his harshly beautiful face.

"Kiss me, husband," she said. "You could do that forever, if you like."

"Forever it is," Atlas said, his voice still rough. Still raw. "I promise."

But he kissed her as if it was the first time. As if every time would be their first time. Exactly that wondrous, hot and healing. Perfect in every way.

Theirs, always.

And so it was.

Atlas saw to it personally, just as he'd promised her. Forever.

CHAPTER THIRTEEN

ELEVEN YEARS LATER Atlas stood out on that same bluff in Martha's Vineyard and watched the sailboats in the distance, tacking back and forth as they headed upwind.

He remembered that long ago day when he'd found Lexi here, frightened and defiant in turn. He remembered the things they'd said and the way they'd fought their way to each other as clearly as if it had happened yesterday.

But so much had happened since.

It had taken longer than it should have to gather enough evidence to prove what Atlas had long suspected, that Richard had been the one to choke his own daughter before dropping her in the pool that Lexi had long since had removed from the property. There was a flower garden where it had stood, fragrant and colorful blooms to celebrate Philippa's life rather than mourn her death.

Lexi called that moving on.

Atlas liked the flowers. But he much preferred visiting the old man in prison where he belonged.

"Have you come to gloat again?" Richard had asked the last time he'd made the pilgrimage to the prison that had swallowed up a decade of Atlas's life. "What a petty man you are."

Atlas had only smiled. "You never have told me why you did it. Why you killed your own daughter."

Richard looked older. Diminished. But he'd still stared at Atlas with that same flat dislike.

"She defied me," he'd said simply, as if that explained everything.

And perhaps it did. Perhaps, for a man like Richard, obedience was the only thing that mattered. He'd wanted his daughter to marry at his command and she'd refused, so he'd disposed of her.

Atlas preferred his own, far more complicated and textured life. He could hear his ten-year-old son Ari in the distance, shouting out excited directions to his faithful sidekick, eight-year-old Nikolai, as the boys tried to overhead smash each other to death on the tennis court.

And when he turned his head, he saw his lovely wife walking toward him, holding the chubby little hand of their five-year-old, Gabriel.

Everything that mattered was right here. In his heart, in his arms, in this life he and Lexi had built together.

She had taught him forgiveness, and though he would always be a hard man, he tried. After their father's arrest, Gerard and Harry had been left reeling. Gerard and his titled wife still marched along in the genteel misery they seemed to prefer, but even they could manage to lock it up enough to indulge in the family gatherings Lexi had insisted they try to hold.

"Because we get to decide what our family is," she'd told Atlas years ago, with that determination that made him adore her all the more. "Not a sick, old man behind bars. Us."

And so they had.

Even Harry had cleaned up his act. First, he'd stopped drinking. Then he'd actually gotten a job at a London charity, as a figurehead of sorts at first—but these days, he ran the place. He'd married a woman who gazed at him with stars in her eyes and they had two-year-old twins.

"The best gift I've ever received was you sacking me," Harry had told Atlas one Christmas, smiling at his then new wife. "You made a man out of me, Atlas. I won't forget it."

Atlas certainly didn't.

He'd been locked up for ten years and he'd thought that the day he'd left prison was the day he'd been set free, but it wasn't. He'd carried his cell with him. He'd locked himself and Lexi in it and he'd had no intention of ever letting either one of them out. He'd stranded himself behind bars of hatred and revenge instead of iron, hurt and loss and fury.

He'd promised Lexi eleven years of suffering, but she'd loved him instead.

And everything was different now.

He looked down at the sleeping three-year-old in his arms, his little Theo crashed out after trying to keep up with his brothers. He wouldn't change the ties that bound him now. They didn't make him smaller, meaner, these babies he and Lexi had made and this life they'd claimed, together.

They made him bigger. Boundless.

Because the best revenge of all was living well. Finding happiness despite the darkness. Casting aside doubt and blame and walking into the light, together.

Or doing their best to get there, one way or another.

Lexi came to stand beside him and they both watched as Gabriel squatted down to pull at the grass. Atlas could feel her beside him. The breeze picked up her hair and let it dance between them, trailing over his arm.

"Are you going to tell me or must I drag it out of you?" he asked after a beat or two.

"I'm enjoying the moment," she told him, and smiled when he arched a brow at her. "It's not often I know something you don't."

Her brown eyes danced, and the ways he loved her should have scared him. Maybe they did. But Atlas was used to it now. The enormity of the things he felt for her. The complexity and the depth.

She was pregnant again. They'd agreed this would be the last child. That they'd built the sprawling family they'd always wanted. They'd raised their boys with all the love and laughter they'd never had, and Atlas didn't see that stopping.

It would grow and grow. He was sure of it. The boys would find their own loves out there and that would add to it. There would be weddings, births. Grandchildren to tumble down this same slope of lawn. Atlas's heart was no longer a finite organ, confined to his chest.

It was Lexi. It was each and every one of his sons. It was all of them together.

It was the baby inside her now, with only two trimesters left to go.

This time, Lexi hadn't wanted to wait to see what they'd have. This time, this last time, she'd wanted to know.

So Atlas waited. He held little Theo and he watched Gabriel. He heard the older boys behind him. And he marveled in the sun on his face, the wind in his ears. Things no ex-convict, exonerated or otherwise, would ever take for granted.

"It's a little girl," Lexi whispered, and Atlas felt her fingers curl around his. "We're having a little girl."

"This is what you do, Lexi *mou*," he murmured, lifting her hand to his mouth and placing a kiss there. A sweet, scant promise of the way he'd reward her later, in their bed. When it was only the two of them and that wild heat that only burned hotter between them as time marched on. "You make everything perfect."

Six months later Atlas's only daughter was born into her father's hands on a rainy London morning.

But she brought the sunshine with her, just like her mother, who smiled so wide when Atlas laid the baby on her chest that he thought he would feel it forever. Like some kind of brand, deep inside him, still and always burning bright and hot and red.

"I could not possibly love you more," he told her then.

And Lexi, his beautiful Lexi, smiled even wider.

"You always say that," she reminded him. "And then you do."

Atlas vowed he always would.

Just as he would love his boys, and the tiny, perfectly formed little girl they'd welcomed to the world today, whom he hoped with all his heart would grow up to be just like her mother. Beautiful and maddening, sweet and stubborn, and bright enough to light up a dark and bitter heart like his.

And they named her Philippa, just to make sure.

* * * * *

MILLS & BOON

Coming next month

CLAIMING HIS HIDDEN HEIR
Carol Marinelli

'We were so hot, Cecelia, and we could have been good, but you chose to walk away. You left. And then you denied me the knowledge of my child and I hate you for that.' And then, when she'd already got the dark message, he gave it a second coat and painted it black. 'I absolutely hate you.'

'No mixed messages, then?' She somehow managed a quip but there was nothing that could lighten this moment.

'Not one. Let me make things very clear. I am not taking you to Greece to get to know you better, or to see if there is any chance for us, because there isn't. I want no further part of you. The fact is, you are my daughter's mother and she is too young to be apart from you. That won't be the case in the near future.'

'How near?'

Fear licked the sides of her heart.

'I don't know.' He shrugged. 'I know nothing about babies, save what I have found out today. But I learn fast,' he said, 'and I will employ only the best so very soon, during my access times, Pandora and I will do just fine without you.'

'Luka, please…' She could not stand the thought of being away from Pandora and she was spinning at the thought of taking her daughter to Greece, but Luka was done.

'I'm going, Cecelia,' Luka said. 'I have nothing left to say to you.'

That wasn't quite true, for he had one question.

'Did you know you were pregnant when you left?' Luka asked.

'I had an idea...'

'The truth, Cecelia.'

And she ached now for the days when he had been less on guard and had called her Cece, even though it had grated so much at the time.

And now it was time to be honest and admit she had known she was pregnant when she had left. 'Yes.'

Continue reading
CLAIMING HIS HIDDEN HEIR
Carol Marinelli

Available next month
www.millsandboon.co.uk

LET'S TALK

Romance

For exclusive extracts, competitions
and special offers, find us online:

Or get in touch on 0844 844 1351*

For all the latest titles coming soon, visit
millsandboon.co.uk/nextmonth

*Calls cost 7p per minute plus your phone company's price per minute access charge

Want even more
ROMANCE?

Join our bookclub today!